Emily Sneller

NO PROMISES

NO PROMISES

PAMELA CURTIS SWALLOW

G. P. PUTNAM'S SONS ➤ NEW YORK

ACKNOWLEDGMENTS

Sincere thanks to my editor, Anne O'Connell.

Library of Congress Cataloging-in-Publication Data
Swallow, Pamela Curtis.
No promises / by Pamela Curtis Swallow. p.   cm.
Summary: The new French student at school has a totally
different approach to life than fifteen-year-old Dana,
but despite a certain amount of jealousy on the part of
her boyfriend and a girlfriend, Dana forms a very special,
rewarding relationship with Jared.
ISBN 0-399-21561-1   [1. Friendship—Fiction.]   I. Title.
PZ7.S969895No   1988   [Fic]—dc19   88-2702   CIP   AC

For Devin
and
in memory of J.R.

NO PROMISES

Chapter One

He was sitting at the desk behind mine when I walked into geometry class one Monday afternoon in the middle of October.

"Hi," he said, smiling. I'd never seen eyes like his before. Not eyes that full of life.

I was surprised to see a new student coming into the class so far along into the marking period. "Hi," I answered, slipping into my chair.

Lynn turned around in her seat in front of mine. Grinning, she held up a scrap of paper with "Cute!" written on it. As she started to talk, I could tell she was self-conscious. "So, Dana—boring weekend, huh. You didn't see Paul at all?"

"No, his family went somewhere in Massachusetts to visit relatives and he had to go with them. But the weekend wasn't a total loss. I made some money baby-sitting and went shopping. And I got some of the English project done."

"What'd you buy?" She snuck another quick look at the new boy.

"Sweatpants and shorts—nothing exciting, just stuff I needed for gym," I answered.

"Let's walk to town after school," Lynn suggested.

"Sorry, can't. I have to exercise Dusty. It was so wet this weekend, I didn't ride." Looking out the window I could see the ground was still a little muddy. I'd have to stick to the upper pasture.

I felt a tap on my shoulder. "You ride?" The new boy's voice was kind of low and mature sounding.

"Yes," I said, turning around. I got a better look at him this time. Lynn was right—he *was* cute. Along with the green eyes you couldn't miss, he had thick black hair and a face that a sculptor would like—an angular sort of handsomeness. He was fairly thin, but not skinny.

"Your own horse?" he asked. Shy he wasn't.

"No, my neighbor's. I just take care of him. The girl he belongs to is away at college."

"I used to ride. We had horses in France," he said.

Lynn's eyes widened. "You lived in France? Really . . . or are you kidding?"

From the quizzical expression on his face it was hard to tell.

Lynn looked doubtful.

"Really," he said.

"I don't believe you," Lynn said.

Suddenly he was spouting something in French; I knew enough French to recognize "chevaux," so I could tell he was talking about horses. His accent was terrific. It sounded just like the pronunciation tapes my teacher played.

My face must have looked startled. He laughed and said, "I'd like to ride with you sometime."

"My name is Lynn," she piped in.

I don't think he heard her. He just said, "All right?" looking at me.

I nodded slowly, staring back into his incredible eyes. Suddenly I blushed and said, "You speak French so well. You obviously won't have to take French here." I wondered if he was purposely trying to impress us, or if he was just matter-of-factly making a point.

"My French teacher would be embarrassed to have you in the class—you're too good," Lynn said.

Mr. Dougall stood up from his desk at the front and said, "All right, let's get going. Take out the weekend's homework, please." He paused, taking off his glasses. "Before I forget my manners—we have a new transfer student, Jared Rochet, joining us today. Jared, we're on page ninety-eight, working with direct proofs."

Mr. Dougall walked down our aisle and handed Jared a book. "Please see if you can follow what we're doing. You may or may not have already covered this material in your previous course."

Jared nodded as he took the book.

"I'll speak with you after class about whether you're in the right section," Mr. Dougall went on. "There are a couple other geometry classes to consider if this one seems wrong." He turned to write on the board. There was a chalk smudge on his pants.

"I'll talk to you later about riding," Jared whispered to me.

Boy, he moves fast, I thought. I wondered how old he was—a sophomore like I was, or a junior? The class was a

11

mix, depending on how advanced the students were and in what order kids had taken their math courses. He seemed older than a lot of the boys, so I guessed he was a junior.

For the rest of the period, I was very aware of his being behind me. I was certain those eyes were on me.

"Want to change seats?" Lynn asked as we walked out of class. "It really isn't fair, you know. I saw him first, and you already have Paul." She jabbed me with her elbow, and grinned. "I'm stopping at the office to see if they need me to start a welcome committee. You know—to make new students feel more at home. I can be very, very welcoming."

"Yes, you can," I said, laughing, "and you, as founder of the welcome committee, are *welcome* to come riding the day he does."

"Thanks! Count me in. I've always loved Dusty."

"You're *welcome*. But you can't fool me *or* Dusty. You haven't exactly been a devoted fan of his since the day he nipped your behind when you were mounting. And then when you finally got on, he bucked you off, remember?"

"I can forgive, forget, and fake it when it comes to an opportunity to see a cute guy," Lynn said, giggling.

"You better make your move fast. We don't even know if he's going to stay in our class. I didn't hear anything he and Mr. Dougall were saying after class, did you?"

"No, but my fingers and toes are crossed. So far he's the best part of geometry," Lynn said.

We reached the hall intersection. Lynn's last class was art, down the hall to the left. I had band, to the right. "Have fun tooting your horn. I'll talk to you tonight," Lynn called as she darted into the stream of students moving left.

I hurried to the band room, dropped my books by my instrument locker, and took out my mellophone. We had drill outside on the football field and most of the people were already out there. I had to hustle or my drill captain would scream. By this time in my life I should have been used to getting yelled at for being late—it's what I usually was.

For October it was pretty warm. Standing at attention, I wished I'd gotten rid of my sweater before running onto the field. We stood for a long time while the two band directors talked up in the press box. I glanced across to where Paul was standing. He was one of the leaders of the band, and even though he was a junior, he got more respect than the senior who was band president. Everyone knew what an excellent musician he was. The directors wrote solos just to show him off. Paul wasn't conceited about his talent, though; he handled it in a modest way.

A bee landed on the bell of my horn and started to walk toward my face. We're not allowed to move when we're at attention, so there was nothing I could do except watch it and listen to it buzz. My eyes must have practically crossed as it crept close to my nose. I felt sweatier than ever as I imagined it stinging my nose and making it swell to the size of a football. With tiny puffs, I tried to blow it away. But it was a sturdy bee. It didn't budge; it stopped and stared at me. I tried to remember if bees have lots of eyes, or if flies do. If we would have just started playing, I could have blasted it away.

Suddenly I jumped as a hand swept past my nose and flicked the bee away. Alec, my squad leader, laughed and walked back to his place in the formation. Drill captains and squad leaders are allowed to move—we little people aren't. Alec's a friend of Paul's, which is probably why he was being nice. I'd thank him later.

We finally began to play. My sneakers had practically become stuck to the muddy spot where I'd stood so long, and I nearly left them behind when I started to march. We were playing "Fascinatin' Rhythm," and I got chills when I heard Paul's trumpet solo. There was no doubt it would be a showstopper when we competed.

When drill was over, I plopped onto the grass and pulled my sweater off. I shook my hair and held it up off my neck for a minute. Paul was talking to the band directors, but he gestured for me to wait.

I watched Paul for a minute. I loved the way he looked, with his blond hair that fell over his ears slightly, and his dark blue eyes. I even liked his eyebrows that sometimes made him look worried even when he wasn't. Though he wasn't particularly tall, he was very strong and had terrific arms.

Paul jogged over to me and we walked back to the band room together. He put his arm around my shoulder. "I thought I'd be able to see you after school, but I have two lawns to rake—they should have been done on Saturday."

"No problem. I have to ride anyway." Although I knew we both had things we had to do, I was disappointed that we couldn't see each other even for just a short time.

"I missed you this weekend," Paul said, taking my instrument and carrying it the rest of the way for me.

"This was one of the few Mondays I looked forward to," I said. "It was weird not seeing you over the weekend. Saturday was okay, but Sunday really dragged."

14

The band room was cool. I'd have liked to stay in there awhile, but I tossed my sweater over my shoulders, picked up my books, and got ready to leave. Paul squeezed my hand and leaned forward to kiss me just as one of the directors walked into the room. "Oh, well, next time," he said softly. "I'll call you later. We can plan something for the weekend."

"Good." I smiled and headed out through the parking lot toward the street.

As I reached the bottom of the driveway, I heard someone whistling. I looked and saw Jared leaning against a white sports car. I couldn't remember ever seeing a car just like that—it looked pretty old.

"Going home?" he asked.

"Yes . . . finally. That felt like the longest last period ever," I answered.

"Want a ride?" he asked.

I hesitated. I really didn't know Jared, and basically I was the cautious type. "Oh, it's nice out. I should walk really. But thanks, anyway." The truth was, it was hot and I was pooped. A ride in a convertible would have felt great. But no. I, Dana goody-two-shoes, straight-arrow, true-blue, sensible McGarren, all sticky and thirsty, would trudge virtuously home alone.

Chapter Two

As I started to walk away, he said something in French. I heard the word "coquette."

"Not again. That's not fair," I said, laughing. "My French isn't good. What did you say?"

He grinned and began to whistle again.

"What'd you say?" I repeated.

He continued to whistle for a moment, then smiled. "I said you were being coy."

"Oh," I started walking again, feeling a little embarrassed. I thought I knew what coy meant but I wasn't positive, and I didn't want to ask him. "Bye, see you tomorrow." I waved over my shoulder.

As I walked down South Avenue I thought about Jared. There was something about him . . . I guess it was the way he seemed to be teasing. He was certainly different from Paul, who's so straightforward.

Paul and I had started going out over the summer, after

we'd gotten to know each other last year in band. That's the only class we've ever had together. A lot of girls like Paul, and I feel very special when I'm with him.

I was walking along with my head down, still thinking about Paul, wondering when we'd be able to go out—Friday, maybe—when I heard the whistling again. I looked up and saw the white sports car parked on the corner in front of me. A hand reached up from the inside and waved. Then Jared sat up, tipped an invisible cap and said, "Are you sure I can't give you a lift?"

I laughed. "No, really, I like to walk. But thanks." I lied well.

"Comme vous voudrez," Jared said as he started the motor. He tipped his invisible cap again and drove off.

"As you wish?" I thought that was how that translated. Close anyway. Where would he pop up next—or had he decided to give it up? I half expected him at the next corner, but he wasn't there . . . nor at the next two. I listened for the whistling, but didn't hear any.

My books were feeling really heavy by the time I turned up my street. I shifted them in my arms and to distract myself, I began to run through our band drill in my head, humming my part. As I rounded a curve in the road, I was startled to hear, "Thirsty?"

A hand, holding a 7-Up, rose up out of Jared's car, parked on the shoulder of the road. As I got closer I could see Jared slouched lazily in the seat. This is one persistent Frenchman, I thought.

"Thank you," I said, laughing as I reached for the can and took a long drink. "How'd you know where to go? You don't know where I live, do you?"

17

Jared sat up and grinned. "Call me Sherlock." Then he began to whistle again.

"What is that you keep whistling, anyway?" I asked.

"I'm a terrible whistler, but hang on a minute. I can do better with this." He reached around to the backseat and pulled up a battered guitar case. Then, not having enough room with the steering wheel in front of him, he got out of the car and leaned against the fender. Gently he opened the case and took out a beautiful guitar, all inlaid with ivory and different shades of wood. He carefully tuned it for a moment, then, leaning there on his car by the side of the road, he began to sing in a low, rich voice. It was a French song. I could understand only parts of it, but it was beautiful.

If anyone else had done that—suddenly whipped out a guitar and started to sing to me—I'd have laughed hysterically. But for some reason, it didn't seem weird or corny when Jared did it. He had an unusual style. No one I knew was the slightest bit like him.

I began feeling silly about not accepting his ride. A person who played the guitar like that and sang beautiful French songs wasn't likely to be Jack the Ripper. Besides, Jared was in my class and since we were only a short distance from my house, I climbed into his car and we drove the rest of the way together. The seats were very low; I felt a little self-conscious about sitting so close to him and in such a low position as we barely skimmed the road. But the breeze felt good. My legs were stretched out in front of me, tucked between soda cans, paperback novels, and Reese's peanut butter cup wrappers.

I pointed to my driveway a little late and Jared had to swing sharply to make the turn. Gravel flew to the side, landing in my mother's flower bed. I knew I'd have to get it out of there later.

Jared turned off the motor, and like a pop-up toy, my brother, Rex, poked his head out the back door. "Hey, great!" he said, eyeing the car. "What is that, anyway?"

"An MG," Jared answered.

"I never saw one like that."

"It's an old one."

Rex walked around the car. He ran his hand over the fender. "How old?"

"Probably older than you. How old are you?" Jared asked.

"Eleven . . . twelve really soon," Rex answered.

"She's got you beat."

"She?" Rex laughed. "How can you tell it's a she?"

"Can't you? Look at her. Mignonne—no doubt about it," Jared answered.

Rex looked bewildered. Jared explained, "Mignonne means pretty in French."

Rex nodded, seeming to accept Jared's explanation.

Now that Jared was at my house, I guessed I should invite him in. "We can get something to eat inside, but we'll probably have to be quiet. A neighbor of ours had a stroke, and my mother helps him with his speech a couple of afternoons a week—I think this is one of the days."

We went into the kitchen. The door into the dining room was closed, so I knew Mom was in there with Mr. Randall. On the kitchen table was a note. "Hi Rex and Dana—I'll be through at 4:30. Have a snack. Love, Mum." I smiled. She always leaves a little greeting if she's going to be busy. It's nice.

"The hermits are good," Rex remarked, letting the screen

19

door slam behind him as he headed for the refrigerator and took out the milk. "They're in the tin over by the toaster."

Jared looked in the direction of the toaster. I guessed that he wasn't sure what a hermit was.

"They're cookies—want one?" I reached for the tin and passed it to him.

He peered in. "They're good," I said. "It's my grandmother's recipe. They have raisins."

"Thanks."

"Does the car belong to you?" Rex asked. "Or is it your parents'?"

Jared chewed and swallowed. "My brothers had it first. Now it's mine."

"Lucky," Rex said. He stood looking at Jared for a moment, as if he wanted to ask more, but maybe wasn't sure what. "Well, I guess I'll watch some TV while Mom's too busy to know I'm doing it." He sauntered over to the steps leading down to the family room. "See you."

"I'm really sorry, Jared," I said, as Rex disappeared down the stairs. "That was my brother, Rex. I never introduced you."

"I figured out who he was—no problem. He's the first Rex I've ever known."

"Named after my uncle Rexford. Sounds more like a dog or a dinosaur but, oh well . . ." I said, laughing, "we all like the name."

I didn't know what to do next. There I was in my kitchen with a boy I hardly knew, who was probably expecting to go riding. And I'd told Lynn I'd include her. What now?

I'd try small talk. "Where'd you go to school before?"

"Stratfield Academy," he answered.

"That's a prep school, isn't it?"

"Uh-huh."

"Did you board there or were you a day student?"

"Bored, as in b-o-r-e-d," he said laughing. "I lived there. My parents have a theory, I think, or at least a tradition, that teenagers should be AWAY. Everyone gets along better that way. My two older brothers went, and I have a younger sister who's a freshman at Chatham Hall."

"What happened? Why'd you end up at the high school?"

Jared chuckled. "My parents and Stratfield came to an agreement—that I was wasting Stratfield's time and my parents' money."

"Were you?"

Jared shrugged. "In their opinion, maybe. I was learning, I was studying even, but not when and what they wanted. To me, an education is a personal thing. But I can go ahead with it here as well as there, so it doesn't matter."

"Our high school isn't bad—I'm sure you'll be able to find teachers and kids you'll like," I said. I was feeling a little defensive about my school.

He winked. "I already have."

I could feel my face getting red. I thought about Paul and changed the subject. "Where do you live?"

"On Chestnut Ridge—the old stone house with the barn behind it. We moved there about a year and a half ago and I've been trying to talk my parents into using the barn for a horse ever since. They don't think any of us are home enough, though. My mother's sure she'd be left doing the work."

"Didn't you say you had horses in France? Did you really live there?" I asked.

"We still do in the summer. Our family's business

21

is there. My father and my uncle export French perfume and soap." Jared reached for another cookie. "When I was younger, we lived there most of the year and just came here for the summer. But now it's the other way around." He took another bite and chewed. "The horses were sold," he said finally.

"You don't have much accent," I commented.

"I've been in the States so much, it's pretty well gone."

The dining room door opened and my mom popped her head into the kitchen. "Oh, hi," she said smiling. "I wasn't sure who was here. I thought I heard a voice I didn't recognize."

"Mom, this is Jared . . . Oh, I'm sorry. I've forgotten your last name," I said, embarrassed.

"Rochet." He crossed the floor and shook my mother's hand.

For a brief instant I thought he might kiss it in a gallant European manner, but I guess I only thought that because he was French.

"Jared's new at school," I added.

"Nice to meet you, Jared. I'll be done pretty soon, Dana." Mom closed the door.

"So, are you going to ride now?" Jared asked.

"Um, I should really. But I told Lynn she could join me. I'll see if she's home yet." I reached for the wall phone and dialed Lynn's number. No answer. "No one's there."

"Is Lynn your friend from geometry?" Jared asked.

"Yes. She said something about wanting to ride, but she also said something about going to town on her way home. Maybe she found a sale. She's a real shopper."

I stood there, leaning against the counter, feeling self-conscious and trying to figure out what to do next. I guessed the easiest thing was just to go riding as I had planned, and not feel guilty about being in a situation I *hadn't* planned.

"You feel okay about riding in those?" I asked, pointing to his school clothes.

"They're not exactly the best for the occasion, but I've been known to wear worse," he said, smiling.

"Well, excuse me for a minute, all right? I have to change. Help yourself to something more if you're still hungry. I'll be right back." As I opened the door into the hallway my cat strolled into the kitchen. "You can chat with Pip while I'm gone."

"Well, Pip," I heard Jared say, "it's nice to make your acquaintance. I think you and I may become good friends."

Chapter Three

We walked up the hill of the lower pasture toward the stable. Dusty was nowhere in sight, so I whistled for him. As we reached the top of the hill we saw him trotting toward us. He must have been over by the apple trees near the driveway.

"He's good-looking," Jared said, smiling.

I snuck a sideways glance at Jared and thought the same thing about him.

Dusty reached us and nuzzled my arm, looking for sugar. I'd forgotten to bring any. "Sorry, Dusty—next time."

Jared stroked Dusty's neck. "Why's he called Dusty? His coat is such a rich, pure chestnut."

"It's short for Stardust—from the song with that name," I answered, watching Jared make friends with Dusty. Most of the kids who ask to come riding with me aren't really very comfortable with Dusty, probably because of his size. They usually end up climbing up on the fence and perching there.

"Okay, boy, let's get you ready," I said. Dusty followed as we walked to the stable and he waited by the tackroom door as I took his bridle down from its peg. "Hold still," I said. He was playing his usual game of being difficult. As soon as I'd taken his halter off, he tossed and dodged his head so that it was practically impossible to get the bridle on. I finally slapped him on the neck, and when he saw that I'd had enough of his antics, he held still. He must have wanted exercise, because he opened his mouth and took the bit the first time, rather than clamping his teeth together the way he usually did.

"Jared, if you'll hold him, I'll get the saddle on." I went back into the tackroom and took the saddle off the rack. When I first began taking care of Dusty, I cleaned the tack practically every day. I wasn't quite so gung-ho now but I'd have to remember to clean it this week—it definitely needed it. I tossed the saddle pad on first, then the saddle. When the girth was tight, I reached for the reins. "I think I'd better try him out first, before you get on, to see what sort of mood he's in."

I put my foot in the stirrup and swung up. Dusty was eager to take off. I held him back as we trotted close to the pasture fence. I slowed him to a walk as we went down the hill. I knew what he'd do when we reached the bottom, and I was right—he spun around and took off like a rocket up the hill.

As we neared Jared, I laughed. "This is why I went first. He acts this way when he hasn't been ridden in a while. I'll take him down the hill once more and then give him to you."

Jared nodded. "Fine." He leaned against the fence and watched me turn Dusty and head back down the hill.

After I thundered up the hill once more, I hopped off and handed the reins to Jared. "He's a little temperamental, but if he thinks you're not afraid, he's usually all right. Show him who's in charge."

"I'm not worried. I had a horse a lot like this once," Jared said, adjusting the stirrups. He swung up into the saddle in one smooth, powerful move. He squeezed Dusty's sides and trotted off across the field. Effortlessly he eased Dusty into a gentle canter. He looked very comfortable riding. It was obvious he had not made up the story about having horses.

I climbed to the top rail of the fence. After about ten minutes Jared called, "Are there any trails we could go on?"

"Yeah," I answered, "but I don't think there's time today. I have two tests to study for. Besides, it's still too muddy."

"Okay," Jared said, turning Dusty around and reversing his course. "Maybe some other time." He rode awhile longer. Then I took one more turn.

We talked while we took off Dusty's saddle and bridle and then fed him. "You're lucky to have the privilege of riding any time, but not having the bills that go with having a horse," Jared commented.

I thought it was interesting that he used the word "privilege"—I liked that. "It's a good deal," I admitted. "I can even use Dusty to give lessons and earn some money. I did that last summer."

"Not bad. So," he said, changing the subject, "who's Paul?" He sat down on a bale of straw and leaned back, waiting for my reply.

"What?" I hadn't expected the question. "Oh, he's the guy I'm going out with. How'd you hear about him?"

"Your friend in geometry class said something."

"Oh, yes. She asked about the weekend," I said.

"What's he like?"

"Nice . . . nice to everyone . . . and athletic . . . and very musical. He plays solos in the band," I said, picking up a brush off the floor, "and has his own small group that plays at parties." I started toward the door. "Dusty's done eating. I think I'll brush him for a minute before we go."

Jared took another brush from the shelf and came out with me. "What kind of music does Paul play?"

"All types. Some rock, but usually jazz and Dixieland. He's very talented," I said definitely. Dusty liked being brushed and stood still while we each took a side.

"Classical guitar is my thing. But not too many people our age are into it," Jared said.

"Is that one of the things you were studying at Stratfield, when they expected you to be doing something else?" I worked on getting some snarls out of Dusty's mane.

"One of several things I was doing, yes. I was also reading a lot—Fitzgerald and Sartre mainly. The problem was that the assignments seemed shallow and brief. I couldn't get into things as much as I wanted . . . so the classes would move on, and I wouldn't," he said, laughing.

"I've always thought that it was crazy that while people are supposed to be getting educated, there usually isn't time for them to really learn things well enough to feel as if they are actually *being* educated," I said. "It's all so rushed."

Jared nodded. "Right." At the same time, we both reached to brush Dusty's back and our arms bumped. I glanced quickly at Jared and saw him smile at me.

"Oops. You do the front part, I'll do the back," I said,

27

hoping I didn't look embarrassed. I couldn't help noticing his tanned, strong-looking hands.

Dusty was in heaven with all the attention and looked sorry to see us stop. As we started across the field toward my house, Jared asked, "You know what I'm interested in; what interests you?"

"Well, I'm not positive what I want to concentrate on, for the future, that is. Maybe psychology. But right now I like writing. I wish there was more chance to do it in school, but I guess it's too much work to correct. Most of my teachers stick with multiple choice."

We heard barking from the direction of my house. "Sounds like Bernie," I said. "Our dog. Mom must be done helping Mr. Randall. She usually keeps Bernie in her bedroom out of trouble while she's working."

Jared glanced toward the house. "What kind of dog?"

"Dachshund—but don't let his size fool you. He's a real handful. If he isn't closed up in Mom's room when there's no one to keep an eye on him, there's no telling what he'll do."

"That little guy?" Jared said, pointing to the small black dog running up the hill to meet us. Bernie's ears flapped and his license tags jingled as he ran on his stubby legs.

"Yup, this guy," I said, kneeling down. I picked Bernie up and carried him as we walked the rest of the way to the house. "Yesterday he was really a devil. Remember how lousy it was out?"

"Yeah?"

"It was raining so hard that after church Rex didn't want to walk Bernie, so he just let him out. He forgot to keep an eye on him." As I rattled on, I began to feel a little silly, but

I kept going. "Later, I opened the back door to call him, and I found the steps covered with boots—all shapes and sizes." I started to laugh.

"Boots?" Jared grinned.

"About eight or nine of them!"

"Where'd they come from?"

"Bernie took them off neighbors' porches. It took us ages to call people and trudge around pulling a wagon full of boots, to get them all back to the right people." I looked at Jared, relieved that he was laughing. I'd have felt pretty stupid if he'd just been staring at me blankly while I went on and on about my dog.

We went into the house through the mudroom. Rex called from upstairs, "Dana, Paul wants you to call."

"Okay." I saw Jared glance at me quickly, then look down at Bernie.

"Bernie, old boy, you're quite a guy," Jared said. Bernie jumped up and put his front paws on Jared's knees. Jared reached down and stroked Bernie's head. "The afternoon was fun, Dana. Thank you for letting me join you. I've really missed riding."

"I would, too. I do a lot of thinking and relaxing when I'm with Dusty." I bent down to pat Bernie too, then felt Jared looking at me, and straightened up.

"Maybe it isn't hopeless to try to convince my parents to let me have a horse again, especially now that I'm going to school here. The summer is the problem—we're only here for about a week of it." He leaned back against the counter.

"If I had a barn, the property, and the money, I'd certainly keep working on it," I said.

"You're right—I will." He hesitated for a moment.

29

"Well, see you in geometry. I guess I'll stay in that class. Mr. Dougall asked me what I thought. I didn't say I'd had most of it already." He grinned. "But since I don't plan to spend much time on math anyway, I ought to be able to pass."

"And still have time for Fitzgerald," I added, laughing.

"You've got it. Well, gotta go. Go make your phone call." Jared winked, and backed out through the door. "A bientôt!"

Chapter
Four

As I watched Jared hop into his car and drive off, a few measures of his song ran through my head. Mom came into the kitchen and began poking around in the refrigerator. "That boy seems nice," she remarked. "You said he's from school?"

"Yeah. He transferred from Stratfield Academy. Today was his first day. Need any help?"

"Not yet, thanks. I'll call you," Mom answered. "But tell Rex to feed Bernie and Pip. I'm going to trip over them any second."

I headed upstairs. Rex was on his bed counting money. "Hey, you're loaded," I said. "Where'd it come from?"

Rex grinned. "I love counting money when I have a lot. Dad sent me some for my birthday, which is *next* Friday, I want you to know."

"I know, I know," I said, mussing his hair. Actually, I hadn't realized it was getting that close. I'd have to walk to town one day after school and get something. "How much do you have, Moneybags?"

"Forty-six fifty." He flicked his eyebrows up and down, reminding me of Fagin in *Oliver*.

"Lucky," I said, wondering about my own money situation. "Mom said to tell you that Bernie and Pip want to dine. They're being nudgy."

"All right. One minute," Rex stalled.

I went into my room and checked the envelope at the bottom of my sock drawer. The money supply didn't look good. Maybe Mom would loan me a bit so that I could get Rex something decent. I wished Dad had sent me a few dollars, too. But he had no real reason to—my birthday was in June.

Dad moved out and went to California when I was only three and Rex was just a few months old. I don't even remember very well what it was like when he lived with us. But we do see him a couple weeks a year. Every now and then I wonder what it would be like if he were still here. I can't really say that I miss him anymore, because I'm so used to the way things are now. I do like visiting him, though.

Mom, Rex, and I don't have a lot of money, but we're managing all right. Mom teaches nursery school in the mornings, tutors some evenings and in the summer, and she also helps Mr. Randall. I don't even know if she gets paid for working with him. I wouldn't be surprised if she just did it as a friend.

I flopped on my bed and leaned over the side for the phone. For a moment I held the receiver in my hand, then I dropped it back into its holder. I rolled over and stared at the branches outside my window. Until lately it had always been easy to see shapes in the formations of the branches—but now, either the tree was having a growth spurt and the shapes were changing, or I was getting too old to see them. Life was simpler when I could see the shapes.

What a weird day it had been. I was starting to mull it over when Mom knocked on the door.

"We have a choice—for dinner we can have either spaghetti, salad, and garlic bread . . . or we can have hamburgers and French fries." Mom leaned against my door frame and waited for my answer. I liked the way she looked—casual—with her khaki pants and sneakers. Her loose-fitting shirt was the same shade of blue as her eyes. People say she and I look a lot alike. I don't know about that really, but I do know that I wouldn't mind looking the way she does now when I'm middle-aged.

"Umm . . . how about spaghetti and French fries," I suggested.

"No way, you carbohydrate freak," she said, laughing.

"Okay, then—the spaghetti ensemble."

"Fine. I'll call you to do the salad in a while," Mom said, closing the door just as the phone rang.

I leaned over and picked up the receiver. "Hello?"

"Dana," Lynn squealed. "I've got to tell you what happened when I went shopping!" She started to laugh.

"You mean after school?"

"Yeah. I passed a sale sign in front of the new store downtown. Well, you know me and sales—I hustled right in and proceeded to search out the buys." I could tell by her voice that she was trying not to laugh.

33

"I found a huge mound of jumbo-size sweaters piled on a tall standing shelf-thing. There was a top-half mannequin perched on top wearing one of the sweaters. I looked through them, then sat on the edge of the lowest shelf for a minute to tie my sneaker. All of a sudden, the entire mound toppled over, dumping the whole mess of sweaters, *and* the mannequin, on top of me! I was totally buried. The final straw was when the grinning mannequin shifted and whacked me across the face with its hard hand." Lynn started to laugh hysterically.

I couldn't help laughing, too, imagining her groping around under the landslide of wool. Lynn is the sort of person who has things happen to her. But her sense of humor can get her through most anything.

"I had to dig myself out. Do you think anyone offered to help me? Nooooooooo. I had to stand there for AGES re-folding all the sweaters and piling them by colors and sizes. It was a shopper's nightmare!"

"After all that, did you buy anything?"

"Would I let a little calamity like that stop me? Real shoppers plow on. I got a sweatshirt—bright yellow. Did you ride this afternoon?"

"Uh-huh." I hesitated, uncertain whether or not to mention that Jared had come over. If I didn't tell her and she found out later, it would be bad. She might think I intended to see him without her.

"Remember that new boy, Jared?" I sounded stupid trying to be casual about it. I knew perfectly well she remembered him.

"Are you kidding—forget *him*?"

"Right. Well, I tried to call you after school to let you

know that he came over to go riding," I said. "I wanted you to come over, too."

"I don't believe it. He came *today*, right after he met you? Wow, that was fast. What's he really like?"

"Well, I'm not sure I know yet." I rolled over on my back and thought. "He's different. You'll see what I mean. We'll rig it up so that you're here next time. And wait till you see his car—a little white MG."

"Oooh, neat. Does Paul know he came over? I mean, will he mind?"

I sighed. "I think he'll understand. I didn't invite Jared over. He just came. Paul won't mind," I said firmly.

"Probably not. But Dana, you've *got* to promise to get me there the next time Jared comes over—seriously—promise," Lynn said. Then she added, "Of course, it probably wouldn't make any difference anyway."

"What?" I asked.

"I come out looking pretty blah next to you," Lynn said.

"Oh, come on. There's nothing wrong with your looks, plus, you've got an outstanding personality. And don't forget your hair. It's a great auburn shade and has lots of wave."

"Nice try, Dana. But my face is too round and my figure is too . . . umm, I guess the word is sturdy, or something. My hair is curly frizz most of the time. Yours could be in a commercial. I can outflaw you any day."

"Lynn, no one's ever satisfied, me included. I've always wanted to be a blond . . . a blond with brown eyes, instead of a brunette with blue eyes."

"People should be able to make a wish and change one

35

thing about themselves," Lynn said. "But since it doesn't work that way, let's just change the subject."

I wished Lynn could see her own good qualities as well as I could. I sighed. "Okay. Did you start studying for English and chemistry yet?"

"Hold it. You didn't tell me anything about what happened when Jared was over. Come on, what did you do?"

"Just rode Dusty. That's all," I said.

There was a knock on my door and Rex stuck his head in. "You're on. Mom says we have to have roughage. I asked her to explain. She said things that crunch. The peanut crunch bar I had after school wasn't good enough for her, so you have to make a salad." He pulled his head back into the hall, like a turtle into its shell, and closed the door.

"Did you hear Rex? I've gotta go make a salad. If I can, I'll call you later." I knew I probably wouldn't, though. I wasn't in very good shape as far as chemistry went. Periodic tables don't thrill me. It would be a long night.

Halfway through the pile of spaghetti, Rex cleared his throat. I knew something was coming. "Uh, Mom. Can I ask you a favor?" Rex asked. It couldn't be money, I thought; he had more than Mom and I put together.

"Sure. What?"

"Well, in the morning when you drop me off at school . . . uh, would you mind . . ." He bonged his fork up and down a few times while he paused and took a deep breath. "Would it be okay if you didn't kiss me?"

"Oh . . . it embarrasses you? I didn't know that," Mom answered, looking as if she were trying not to sound hurt.

"Rex, I kiss Mom good-bye every morning and I'm not embarrassed," I said.

"Of course not. By the time *you* get to school, it's so late no one's around," Rex said.

Mom laughed. "He has a point, Dana. The crowd's long gone." She patted Rex on the shoulder. "No problem. As long as I can give you a quick kiss before we leave home."

"Deal. What's for dessert? Hey, can we get an early start on the Halloween candy? We always have leftovers—we could take care of them now," Rex suggested.

Mom sighed. "I knew I should have hidden the stuff better. Go ahead. Have something, if you must. Dana, what would you like?"

"Umm. Nothing right now. I'll get something later."

In no time, Rex was back, unwrapping a Snickers bar. Just as he was sitting down, he dropped a Hershey's Kiss on the floor. Bernie made a dive for it. Rex was on top of him in a flash, tugging and yanking on Bernie's muzzle, prying open his mouth and saying rude things to him.

"Easy, Rex. Not so rough," Mom said.

I leaned over and peered under the table. There, lying next to the table leg, was the chocolate kiss. I picked it up, poked Rex in the shoulder, and handed it to him.

"Ooops. Sorry Bernie," he said, releasing the insulted-looking dog who slinked away, giving one backward glance to be sure the chocolate was really off the floor.

Mom got up and carried some dishes to the sink. The phone rang. "It's Paul," Mom called. "If you still have homework, please keep it short."

"Okay," I answered on my way up to my room, taking

37

the stairs two at a time. I flopped on my bed and grabbed the phone. "Hi, Paul."

"Hi. Were you eating?"

"Just finished. I'm sorry I didn't call you back before, but Lynn called, then I had dinner. Did you get the lawns done?"

"Pretty much. How was your ride?"

"I had an unexpected guest." I decided to be straightforward and come out with it. "A new boy from school drove over and rode with me."

"Really? Who?" Paul asked.

"A boy that used to live in France and started the year at prep school. He just came to our school today."

"I know who you mean—he's in my gym class. Jared . . . I forget the last name. I tried to talk him into coming out for cross-country, but he said he hadn't run in a while. So he ended up at your house?" Paul's voice sounded . . . I don't know . . . a little tight, but not exactly angry.

"Yeah, I think in geometry he heard me tell Lynn that I was riding after school, and he likes to ride, so he just came along."

"Should I be jealous?" Paul asked.

My thoughts stopped cold for a second. But then when I realized Paul didn't sound serious, I said, "No, you shouldn't be jealous. And I think you'd like Jared. He's . . . different—smart in an unusual way. He reads a lot and likes classical guitar. Lynn thinks he's great, so we can try to get them together."

"Good idea. Then I can stop bugging Alec to take her out."

"I still think Alec would like Lynn if he'd just give her a chance. She's really fun," I said.

"Yup, she is," Paul said. "But you can't push it. He goes for a different type."

"I know, but he could take a break from cheerleaders just once. He must have gone out with every girl on the squad."

Paul laughed. "Close. Anyway, as long as Lynn is interested in this new guy, you can work on that. Does this fellow like to shop, by any chance?"

"I don't know. Why?"

"It would be a sure sign of compatibility if he did," Paul kidded.

Pip jumped up on the bed and settled in for his after-dinner snuggle. He gets sleepy and affectionate after he eats. He nudged the receiver a few times, trying to get more of my attention.

We talked about other things for a while. With Paul, I never had any trouble thinking of things to say. And I liked listening to him. He had a gentle voice that always made me feel good.

Mom called up the stairs, "It's getting late, Dana. Time to start your homework."

"One minute," I called. "Paul, I gotta go. I have two tests tomorrow."

"Yeah, I should get myself in gear, too. I have a lot of trig. I should also work on that solo I played in band today."

"I thought it sounded terrific," I said.

"Thanks. But it still needs work. I'll meet you by the front door in the morning." Paul said.

"I'll really try to be on time."

"Okay. Have a good night," he said.

"I will. You too. A bientôt," I said as I put the receiver down. Why'd I ever say that?

I got off my bed and dumped my backpack out on the floor. As I flipped through my chemistry notebook, Jared's song ran through my head again. Come on, Dana, I said to myself, get to work. Tonight it's chemistry notes, not musical notes.

Chapter Five

I'd been right—it was a long night. I kept getting my chemical elements mixed up with my compounds, and the substances that were mixtures of one or the other—or both—made it even worse. It was awful how uncomfortable I felt with the whole subject. I was in much better shape for my English test. I'd gone over all my notes on *Our Town* and skimmed the play again. I could relate to that folksy New England world much better than to one made up of test tubes, beakers, and formulas.

Last year biology wasn't much better, but at least there were a few animal-type things to study. Mine never seemed to cooperate though. My planaria, which were *supposed* to be dead, got up and slithered off the slide and down the microscope before I could get a good look at them, let alone answer all the questions on the worksheet. The next week, the earthworm I was given was deformed, with a spinal cord that was all off-center. I had a nice frog, though—

Herb, I called him. I got a little teary when I had to cut him open. Fortunately, unlike my planaria, he was definitely dead.

Tuesday morning, Mom and I took the turn into the school driveway practically on two wheels—our normal style when I'm running late. We're usually just about the only car around by that time, but today a white MG was close behind us. Jared beeped as he passed us, searching for a parking place. My gosh, if I ever had to park, too, at this hour, I'd never make it to homeroom at all.

Paul opened the front door and took my hand as I scooted into the school. "I meant to be on time—really. It's just that I studied for a while before breakfast, then I couldn't find anything to wear."

"It's okay. But I've gotta run. The warning bell already rang," Paul said.

"I know. Thanks for waiting. See you at lunch," I answered. He squeezed my hand, gave me a quick kiss, and took off down the hall toward his homeroom at the far end of the building.

I loved the way Paul was so nice about waiting for me in the morning, and was always so thoughtful . . . carrying things, holding doors.

I was just thinking about whether or not I had time to go to my locker, when I heard a voice behind me. "Bonjour."

"Hi, Jared," I answered, not having to turn this time to know who it was. "I see you have a wee problem with punctuality, too." We headed down the nearly empty hallway together, Jared trailing casually behind.

"Je ne suis pas sujet à l'heure."

42

"What?" I said, shaking my head.

"My time is my own," he said matter-of-factly.

"You may have to work that out with Mrs. O'Grady in the attendance office. She has her own philosophy. I haven't had much influence on her so far." I hesitated at my locker, wondering if I should risk taking the time to leave my jacket and switch some books. I decided to chance it. Bad decision. The bell rang.

"Oh, great," I muttered.

"Not to worry," Jared said.

"You'll start to when you meet Mrs. O'Grady. She'll have you on your knees."

Jared put his hand on my shoulder and shook his head. "Just leave things up to me."

"Bonjour, Madame O'Grady. Comme vous êtes ravissante ce matin," Jared said, in his most charming manner, as we walked into the attendance office.

Mrs. O'Grady's face went from expressionless to beaming. I couldn't believe it. She certainly never beamed at me, or anyone else I knew. Her job was to make you feel *low* for being late, and to give you detention when you'd been late three times.

Jared rattled on about the virtues of patience, understanding, and forgiveness, all the while using a strong French accent. "I, for one, am grateful that you, Madame O'Grady, are indeed kind and understanding, particularly of those of us not fortunate enough to have been born in this land and who sometimes don't understand your American rules . . ."

She continued to smile up at him.

"And this young girl, Madame, was up late into the night—see how weary she looks—studying very hard so that, when the time comes, she might be able to apply to the college of her choice. That is, of course, the goal of all of us serious students." He gave her a winning smile.

Mrs. O'Grady started to speak, but Jared continued. "Now, I ask you, Madame, can you, in your heart of hearts, bring yourself to punish us?"

She sort of squinted her face and shook her pudgy finger at Jared. "You and your young scholar are off this time. We'll let it go this morning." She smiled at him. "Who *are* you, anyway?"

"Jared Rochet."

She didn't have to ask my name, I'd been late so often. She handed us passes.

"Mille fois merci, madame."

We backed into the hall and headed toward our lockers. "You are too much. That woman never gives in to anyone." I began to laugh. "That was some strong accent you used."

"Mais oui. It comes in handy."

"You know, I don't think she counted that as a late time at all. She never put it in her book."

"Of course not. She liked us." He grinned.

As we walked to our homerooms, the loud speaker blared, "ATTENTION PLEASE. GOOD MORNING. WE WILL HAVE A SHORT ASSEMBLY PROGRAM THIS MORNING DURING SECOND PERIOD. REPORT TO THE AUDITORIUM DIRECTLY AFTER YOUR FIRST CLASS."

"Bye, Jared," I said as we came to my homeroom door. "Have a nice day."

"Where were you?" Lynn asked as I walked in and handed my late pass to my homeroom teacher.

I rolled my eyes. "Attendance office. I had trouble getting organized this morning."

"Was that Jared with you?" Lynn asked.

"Yeah. He was late, too."

"God, Dana. You are *so* lucky. You don't even try to see him, but you do. I could probably try like crazy, and *never* see him."

We heard a couple of homeroom announcements before the passing bell rang. "See you in assembly," I called to Lynn as I headed out the door to gym.

I passed several juniors all talking in a cluster. I glanced over my shoulder to see what the big deal was . . . *who* the big deal was, was more like it. I should have known. Jared was in the center of it all. The girls were competing to give him directions to his first-period class. He winked when he saw me pass. I bet he knew perfectly well where the room was.

I hated having gym first period. My hair is never the same afterwards; when I went to the auditorium second period, it felt flat and droopy. Lynn waved. She had a few seats saved. I sat between her and Amy Burg.

"What's this assembly about, anyway?" Amy asked no one in particular, as she dug through her purse and pulled out a nail file.

"Drugs, I think." I looked around, hoping to see Paul. We had to sit in sections by grade, and the juniors got to sit further down front. I caught a glimpse of him coming in a side door with Alec and taking a seat by the aisle.

I wondered where Jared was. Maybe he didn't do assemblies.

A boy I didn't know very well squeezed by us and took the seat next to Lynn. He looked over at her and smiled. She glanced at me and shrugged.

The principal introduced a panel of speakers. I was right —it was a drug program. There were five people on the panel: two adults and three kids not much older than we were.

Just as the speakers were starting, Lynn said in a loud whisper, "Excuse me." I looked over and saw that the boy next to her had put his hand on her knee. She was staring at him, and he was looking right back at her.

"Oh, sorry. I thought you were somebody else," he said. But his hand stayed put.

Lynn cleared her throat. "*Excuse* me." She looked him sternly in the eye. "I *am* someone else."

"Okay." He looked disappointed, and removed his hand. She leaned toward me. "Jeez, what a morning."

The assembly program was good. The adults talked about drug facts and drug penalties. The kids talked about their own experiences and told about how drugs had really messed them up. It was pretty impressive and I think a lot of people really listened to what the kids said.

At lunchtime, I sat down next to Paul and across from Alec in the cafeteria. The smell of hot dogs was in the air. "Hi, Dana. How was your chem test?" Paul asked.

"Yech. I'm never sure how I do on those tests until I get them back. At least I did okay in English." I pulled my sandwich out of my bag, then dug around for my napkin, which was crushed under my apple and my drink. "What are you guys doing?"

"Alec's in charge of the Homecoming Committee. I'm

helping him with some mega-decisions . . . like what food to have at the dance," Paul answered, grinning.

"How about the music?" I asked.

"We've settled that," Alec said. "We have a DJ to do the regular rock. And I've twisted Paul's arm into having his group play some oldies and some jazz."

Lynn walked over to our table, holding an apple in her hand. She leaned over next to my ear and whispered, "Do you see him?"

I knew she must mean Jared. I glanced quickly around the room, then shook my head.

"Rotten luck. He must have second lunch period," Lynn said, taking a bite of her apple and plunking down next to me. She looked at her apple, wrinkled her nose, and added, "Rotten apple, too. It figures. The tree probably had three hundred and eighty perfect ones, and one bad one—and I got it." She sighed and tossed it into the trash.

We all talked until the bell rang, and then headed for our fifth-period classes. I had French. When my teacher spoke, I couldn't help thinking of the French phrases I'd heard Jared speak. I'd love to learn enough to sound half as good as he did. It would really impress "mon professeur."

Lynn was bouncy and sparkly in geometry. I knew it had to do with Jared. Geometry alone did not have this effect on her.

"How'd you like Dusty?" Lynn asked as Jared walked in the door.

"A lot. He has a nice gait," Jared answered. "Do you ride?"

"Sure do." Lynn nodded enthusiastically. "Galloping makes me feel so wild and free," she added.

My shoulders started to shake as I tried not to crack up.

47

Galloping was the last thing Lynn liked to do—it terrified her. A slow trot was her top speed.

Jared took his seat behind mine. He smiled.

"So," Lynn said. "How about a little spin on Dusty this afternoon. I'm up for it . . . anyone else?" She sounded as if she were planning a spin around the block in a sports car.

Jared raised his eyebrows at Lynn. I guessed he knew she wasn't a serious horsewoman. "I'm driving into Manhattan after school," Jared said.

"You're going into New York? After school? Just like that?" Lynn asked in amazement.

"There's a music shop downtown that has great guitar albums and sheet music," he answered.

"I'm lucky if I get to go a couple times a year, and you just zip in any time you want," Lynn moaned. "Where is the justice in this world? All those designer shops . . . those sales racks . . ."

Mr. Dougall opened his book. "Any questions about last night's assignment?" he asked. No one said anything, which was pretty dishonest, if you ask me, because the homework wasn't all that easy . . . at least I didn't think so. Since no one had a question, Mr. Dougall called on two kids, Amy Burg and Brian Stillman, to go to the board and work out the first two proofs.

Reluctantly they went to the front of the room and picked up chalk. Amy looked over her shoulder at her friend Dawn and mouthed, "Oh, nooo. How do you do this one?" It was slow going, and I think both Amy and Brian wished they'd asked questions first.

Jared tapped me on the shoulder. "Do you want to go into the city?"

I turned and looked at him. His eyes were incredible. "What?" I answered, startled by the question. "There's no way I'd be allowed to do that on a school day." I should have added, "Thanks anyway," but I was too surprised by the invitation to think. As I turned around, I felt my face growing hot.

Lynn must have heard, because she turned and looked at us.

Mr. Dougall began discussing the proofs on the board; one was being done correctly, the other wasn't. I was feeling uncomfortable—partly because I might be called on next to do a problem, and partly because of Jared.

Chapter
Six

"Hmmph," said Lynn as we walked to our last-period classes. "I asked, 'where is the justice in this world?' and I meant it. Now, even more."

"Why?" I asked, even though I was pretty sure why.

"First, because Jared can just hop into his little sports car whenever he pleases and visit the shopper's capital of the world—and he probably barely shops—and second, because he didn't even ask me to go along! He asked *you*." She reached out and slapped the wall for emphasis.

I looked at her apologetically.

"You couldn't, or wouldn't, go; I probably could, and would. It figures. This is definitely not my day. Do you think he likes you?"

I had to step aside to avoid being bumped by a football player who wasn't watching where he was walking. "As a friend, that's all. He knows about Paul."

"Good. Talk to you later," she said, as she turned down the hall toward the art room.

I had to agree with Lynn—life isn't fair. But she has a way of rolling with the punches. I'm amazed at how cheery and together she usually is, considering her family situation. It seems as if her parents are almost never home, and when they are, they don't show much interest in her. I think the reason she always has money to shop with is because they figure a big allowance can make up for everything else. I might have only a mom at home, but at least I was rock-solid sure of her love.

I saw Elwood P. Seeds ahead of me in the hall. He's the school's one and only Latin teacher. I loved his name. He's called Mr. Seeds by the other students, but ever since I saw his whole name in the yearbook, he's been Elwood P. Seeds to me, in my head anyway. I worry when he has to navigate the halls. He's kind of frail and could easily get knocked over. I walked faster to get closer. He didn't know me, and had no idea that I always try to walk near him in case he needs someone to catch him. I liked the way he smelled—old-fashioned. I think my grandfather wears the same aftershave.

Paul and Alec were talking to the band directors when I walked into the music room. I got my instrument out of the locker and sat down.

We stayed in for the first ten minutes for announcements and got a pep talk about our first competition. The band to beat had just gotten all new uniforms, new flags, and new drums. We'd have to try extra hard to play well and look sharp.

Paul walked with me out to the field. "Do you know that short little freshman clarinet player, Sheldon?" he asked.

"I think so. Dark curly hair?"

"Yeah. Well, let me know if you see him really getting hollered at. One of the seniors is giving him a hard time."

"I don't think he's on my side of the field. I probably won't see anything," I said.

We did our warm-ups, and then took our positions along the edge of the field and got ready for the entrance. The major blew his whistle, the drums began, and we stepped off. When we reached the spot on the field where we turn, snap up our instruments and begin to play our opening fanfare, I felt a sharp whack on the forehead. My mouthpiece had flown off and practically knocked me out cold. That had never happened before, and I just stood there blinking . . . and probably looking pretty dumb. What was it with this day, anyway?

When we were leaving the field, I saw Paul talking to a senior squad leader. Even from across the field I could tell that Paul was tense. I know his expressions and the way he stands when he's angry. Walking closer, I could hear some of what was being said.

"Get off it, Mark. Give the kid a break," Paul said.

"He's screwing up our rank. He can't march."

"I watched him, and he wasn't that bad. Neither director has said anything, and they don't miss much from up in the stands. They're looking for sloppiness," Paul said.

"Worry about your own section," Mark answered.

I stopped where I was, about five yards away, and waited. Paul mumbled something, turned and walked off the field. I caught up with him. "I was afraid you were going to hit him, Paul."

"Don't think I didn't consider it. The jerk."

"You're nice to stick up for Sheldon," I said.

Paul shrugged. "He's a good player. It would be too bad if he quit because of Mark."

I took hold of Paul's hand and we walked back toward the school. I changed the subject. "Rex's birthday is next Friday. Do you have any ideas for a present?"

"He's starting to get into albums and tapes, isn't he? Maybe you could get him one," Paul suggested. "When I get a free afternoon, I'll go with you to pick one."

"Oh, don't worry about it," I said. With music, running, working, and school, Paul was always so busy. I'd never ask him to shop, on top of everything else. "I'll find out what he likes, then I can get it."

As I was crossing the parking lot to walk home, I saw Mom turn into the driveway. She pulled next to me and leaned over to unlock the passenger door. "I had to do an errand. Thought I'd see if you'd like a ride."

"Thanks," I said, heaving my book bag onto the floor. I leaned back against the seat and sighed. "Phew. Is it a full moon or something?"

"Why?"

"It was a weird day, that's all." I stared out the window and vaguely watched the scenery go by.

Rex had gotten home ahead of us and was already snacking in the kitchen when we walked in.

Mom went to the refrigerator and took out a carton of orange juice. "Want some, anyone?"

"Sure," I said.

"No, thanks," Rex said. "Mom, I've been thinking . . . how about letting me be absent one day next week? You know, sort of a birthday present to me."

"Why?" Mom and I both said at the same time.

"We have a field trip—an historical one. To the same place I went in fifth grade *and* third grade. It's okay once, maybe even twice. But not three times. Jeez, do you suppose they'll hold my senior prom there?"

"You never know," Mom said.

"I know the place you mean—I went a few times, too—and if it was good enough for Washington's headquarters, it should be good enough for your prom," I said, teasing. "They can have a Revolutionary theme."

"Give me a break. I mean the place is bad—the gift shop is the worst. How many postcards and yellowed reproductions of the Constitution can a person use?" He popped another pretzel into his mouth, then flicked it in and out on his tongue, reminding me of a lizard. Finally he bit it. "Why can't they at least have a few snacks . . . you know, 'Ye olde Continental candies' and 'Martha Washington's famous rustic sugar cookies'?"

Mom laughed. "I'll pack you a huge lunch, and I'll include a rustic Ring Ding. Dana, how'd your tests go?"

"English was fine. Chemistry was . . . eh . . . so-so."

"Hey," Rex said. "Is that neat car coming over again today?"

"Nope. Sorry to disappoint you," I answered, reaching in the cupboard for a couple of sugar lumps. "I think I'll ride for a while."

"Good idea. It's a pretty day," Mom answered. "I'm going to do some gardening."

"Oh, by the way, Mom. There's some gravel in the flower bed by the driveway. I'll pick it out for you another time," I said.

*   *   *

Dusty must have been expecting me, because he was standing by the gate near our backyard. As we walked up the hill together, he nosed my pockets and found the sugar.

I opened the tackroom door and went to get the hoof pick to clean out his hooves before I rode. I stared at the shelf where I kept the pick, the brushes, and the currycomb. Someone had moved things around . . . and there was a brand-new brush, an expensive one, sitting on the center of the shelf.

Chapter Seven

Lynn's interest in Jared did not diminish. By the next Monday she'd decided to organize a group to go to a movie and then out to eat. With a bunch of kids going, she figured it wouldn't be too obvious when she asked Jared. He accepted. Then she went nuts worrying and planning.

"What if I don't get to sit by him at the movies?" she said as we were walking to town after school.

"We'll rig it so it has to work out that way, don't worry," I said.

"Someone could shove in front of me or hop over a row of seats and wedge in next to him and screw up the whole seating plan," she went on.

"The only person I know who would hop over a row of seats to sit next to a certain boy is you, so relax. Paul and I will keep an eye out and make sure Jared ends up by you. Besides, it'll probably work out in couples, so there shouldn't be any problem." I stepped around a pile of leaves in the middle of the sidewalk. "Where do you want to go after the movie?" I asked.

"I can't decide whether we should get 'real food' or just dessert. What do you think?"

"We can decide after the show. How many are going, anyway?"

"About six, or maybe seven or eight. Let's see—you, Paul, me, Jared, Amy, Bill, and possibly Dawn and Brian. That's about it, I think," Lynn said.

"Dawn and Brian aren't speaking to each other, so count them out," I commented.

We were almost to town. "Okay, Lynn. We have to switch gears from Friday to today. I want to get Rex a present. And what's the good of my having the champion shopper of all time along if she doesn't have her mind on shopping?"

"All right. Well, I like Paul's idea of a tape or record. And I know the place to go," Lynn said confidently. "Murray's has the best selection and lowest prices."

We found a tape I figured Rex would like. As we were coming out of the store, Jared was just crossing the street toward us, a Coke in one hand and three Reese's peanut butter cups in the other. "Anyone hungry? Thirsty?" he offered.

"No, thanks," we both said.

Lynn smiled at Jared and then looked at his car. "What a great car."

"Thanks. You ladies need a ride?"

"Great!" Lynn's enthusiasm was unmistakable. Without hesitation she tossed her book bag into the back. "Coming?" she asked me.

"No. My mother is meeting me. I'm all set. See you both tomorrow," I said.

Lynn looked puzzled for an instant, then smiled at me. Jared hesitated with his hand on the door handle before he climbed in and they drove off.

I was pretty impressed with my fast thinking, which gave Lynn a chance to be with Jared. It would have been nice if my mother really were coming, though. I shifted my books and started for home.

As I was turning up my driveway and thinking about picking the gravel out of the garden, I heard a car slowing down behind me. Before I turned around, I thought it might be Jared, catching me in my lie. But it was Paul.

"Want a ride?" he said, laughing.

I grinned. "I guess I can manage the next five or six steps on foot." As I watched him pull the large station wagon to the side of the driveway, I thought that anyone who's the least tuned-in to cars (not me) would have known instantly from the sound alone that this was not an MG.

The back door opened and Rex poked his head out. "Hi, Paul. I heard your car." See? I rest my case. Rex's eyes zeroed in on the Murray's bag. "Hey, what'd you buy?"

"Never mind, nosey."

"Ahh right!" Rex shouted. So much for birthday surprises.

When Rex was back inside, Paul looked in the bag. "Good decision. Rex will like that one."

"Between your suggesting it, Lynn finding it, and Mom helping to pay for it, I don't deserve much credit! Except for trudging to town to get it," I said, reaching for the back door. Paul held it open for me.

Rex called from downstairs where he had the TV on, "Hey Paul, how's the track season going?"

"Fine, Rex. Actually, it's called cross-country in the fall. We were supposed to have a meet this afternoon, but the other team's bus broke down."

"I was about to ask you how you got done so early," I said.

Rex called up again. "Hey, could I go to a meet sometime, maybe? I might want to try running when I get to high school."

"Sure. You could come after school next Monday. That's when today's meet is rescheduled for."

"Terrific," Rex shouted. You could hear the excitement in his voice.

I smiled at Paul.

"Rex, where's Mom?" I called.

"Out back. Pruning."

"You were probably planning to ride this afternoon," Paul said. "Right? Come on, I'll go with you."

"You'd be bored, wouldn't you?"

"Nope. I was planning to run today anyway. And I'm dressed for it. Dusty can be my running partner. Get changed and let's go."

"Rex, do me a favor—when Mom comes in, tell her I've gone riding. Okay?"

"Uh-huh," Rex answered.

We took Dusty across the road to the large field that belonged to friends of my mother. The field smelled fresh and the cool air felt good. I started Dusty off at an easy trot, and Paul jogged alongside. The saddle creaked a bit under me. We headed for the trail that led into the woods at the far end. "Is this a good pace?" I asked.

"Fine," he answered, not even puffing. "When we get to the trail, I'll drop behind a ways. I don't think it's wide enough for side-by-side."

"Okay, but be careful he doesn't kick stuff up into your face."

I pulled up on Dusty's reins when we got to a small brook. Dusty always wanted to lunge across, and I wanted to make sure I had him positioned where there weren't many rocks. Paul was about to hop across ahead of Dusty, but I warned him. "Careful—he could leap right on top of you. I don't know why, exactly, but he always makes a big deal out of crossing here. He has a dramatic flair."

Paul stood back while Dusty shifted around, taking tiny steps before making his leap. We both laughed. "See, I told you. He thinks this is a huge gorge or something."

"Hop down for a minute," Paul said, stepping close to Dusty.

I swung my right leg over Dusty's neck and slid down—right into Paul's arms. He pulled me close and kissed me gently. I felt my whole body quiver. But what began as a great romantic moment ended in pain as Dusty nipped me in the seat. I jumped and rubbed the sore spot. "I think he's jealous."

"There's competition everywhere I go," Paul said.

"No there isn't." I wrapped Dusty's reins around a limb and moved out of his reach. Then I put my arms on Paul's shoulders, and we kissed again. After a moment we simply hugged, my head resting on his chest. His strong arms held me almost protectively.

As we stepped apart, Paul tucked some loose hair behind my ear and sighed. "You are *so* beautiful."

"Not in this outfit." I looked down at my worn jeans and frayed sneakers and laughed.

"In anything." He looked into my eyes, and then touched my cheek.

Sitting shoulder-to-shoulder, we talked by the brook for a while. "I wish we could have more time alone together," Paul said, reaching for my hand.

"I know. It seems that we're always so busy, or else we're with a group."

"Let's work at making time for just us." Paul looked at me seriously. "It's important."

"All right, we will."

Paul looked at his watch. "Uh-oh. Speaking of time," he said, "we've run out of it again. It figures. I've got to get going. I told my mom when I took the car that I'd pick up my father at the train station. I'd like to stay here for hours more." He kissed me gently on my forehead.

"We'll come back again," I said, smiling at him.

"Should I just run back, or are you ready to go, too?"

"I'll go back now. I have some jobs to do at the stable anyway."

Dusty was happy to get moving again, especially in the direction of home . . . and supper. I had to hold him back. Paul kept up until we crossed the road and I let Dusty thunder up the final hill. I hopped off at the stall door, and led Dusty around to cool him off while I waited for Paul.

For a minute I thought I heard a sound inside the tackroom. Sometimes mice get in there—maybe one knocked something over. I turned and watched Paul come up the hill. When he stopped in front of me, he leaned over for a minute to catch his breath.

"What time is the train?" I asked.

Paul bent down to pull up his socks. "In about ten minutes—I've gotta hurry."

Then came the whistling. I froze.

Paul looked in the direction of the tackroom. "Do you hear that?" He walked toward the door, while I stood motionless.

Chapter Eight

Paul reached for the door and pulled it open. There was Jared, stretched out on top of a couple bales of hay, with his hands behind his head, whistling.

"Jeez, Jared. What are you doing?" Paul said. He glanced back at me as if to see if I knew.

"I just came to visit Dusty. But he wasn't here, so I figured Dana was riding. I wasn't in a hurry, so I waited."

"I didn't know you were coming," I said.

"No problem," Jared said.

But I could see from the look on Paul's face that there was. He looked at his watch. The train would be in soon and he had to get to the station. He said something under his breath before he reached for my hand, squeezed it, and said he had to go. "I'll talk to you tonight," he said firmly, and walked to his car.

"Nice day for a ride," Jared said. "Would you mind if I just took Dusty around the pasture a couple of times?"

"If you want. But he may not behave too well. He thought he was done. His mind is on food now," I said, trying to figure out how I felt. I was sorry that Paul had gotten so upset, but I wasn't sure whether to be angry at Jared. He probably saw no reason for Paul to be jealous, but he shouldn't have presumed that he could just pop over and ride any time.

"Well, I'll see how it goes." Jared swung up, pressed his legs to Dusty's sides, and went off at an easy canter along the fence. He slowed him to a walk and headed down the hill.

I stood in the same place I'd been since Paul opened the door and discovered Jared. I was still feeling muddled by everything.

Jared controlled Dusty very well as they came up the hill toward me. I'd have bet ten dollars that Dusty would come to a screeching halt right in front of his stall so he could eat, but somehow Jared kept him going right by, as smooth as could be. Jared had the most relaxed body on a horse I'd ever seen.

Unpredictable. Jared was that. And did he know what kind of effect he had? Not just on horses, but on people, too. He left Lynn all nutsy infatuated, me bewildered, and Paul probably furious.

Jared came back up the hill and hopped off. "I should let him eat now," he said, holding the stirrup up and unfastening the girth. When he lifted the saddle off and carried it into the tackroom, I couldn't help noticing his arm muscles. Coming back, Jared had Dusty's halter in one hand and the new brush in the other.

"Here, I'll help," I offered, reaching for the halter. "Dusty nips sometimes."

"He won't," Jared said. And he was right. Dusty was as polite as I've ever seen him. "I'll brush him while he's eating."

"Okay." I wasn't sure Dusty would like that, but I got the feed pail anyway and scooped some grain in. Dusty followed me into the stall and waited while I hung the pail on the hook in the corner.

Jared began brushing. Dusty didn't seem to mind. I felt dumb just standing there, so I went and got the old brush and started on the other side of Dusty's neck. "You were the one who left the new brush here, weren't you?" I asked.

"Yes," Jared said matter-of-factly. I didn't suppose Jared offered explanations unless pressed. Since it didn't seem like a big deal, I just thanked him and let it drop.

"So, you're coming to the movies Friday night?"

"Probably," Jared replied. "Lynn asked me. Would you like a ride?"

"I think I have one. Paul can usually get a car on the weekend. But I'm sure Lynn would like one." I set the brush down. "Just a minute. I want to get something to trim the mane."

I went into the tackroom and stood staring out the window for a moment, thinking. I decided I was a little annoyed at Jared for creating the situation, and I was angry that Paul acted so possessive and maybe even suspicious. But why should I feel guilty? I hadn't done anything and nothing was going on anyway. Besides, I was sure Jared was interested in Dusty more than in me.

I took a deep breath, grabbed the scissors, and went back to Dusty's stall.

After dinner Paul called. "How's everything?" he asked. I could hear the tension in his voice. "I considered dropping my dad off and driving back."

"Everything's fine. Jared rode, I fed Dusty, we brushed him, and I cleaned the tack. Then he left." I tried sounding as bored by it all as possible. I almost added a yawn.

"I thought you were going to get him to see Lynn?"

"He did. He drove her home and she asked him to go to the movies Friday . . . and anyway, Jared came to see Dusty, not me," I said.

"Yup, uh-huh. Same as I did," Paul said.

"You can't equate your visit with his, Paul. Don't be silly. He knows all about you, and he isn't doing anything wrong. He's just a friend. That's all."

"Has he ever . . ."

"Paul! This is stupid. You're making a big deal out of nothing. I didn't invite him. He just dropped by. Can we please change the subject?" I was feeling annoyed that I had to explain something that wasn't my doing and was nothing anyway.

"Okay. Sorry," Paul said.

"Mom is taking Rex and his pals to the movies for his birthday," I said. "Poor Mom."

"I remember going with a bunch of friends at that age. It was pretty noisy," Paul said.

We talked for a few more minutes, then said good-bye. We didn't mention Jared's visit again.

By Friday Lynn was a bundle of nerves. "I've never gone out with a Frenchman before. They're supposed to be such great lovers."

"Relax. It's only a first date—a group one at that—and besides, he's almost as American as he is French," I said, rolling my eyes.

She snapped her fingers. "Heck. Can't win 'em all! Do you think he'll offer to pick me up? What should I do if he doesn't? I'll hate it if he doesn't drive me."

"Then tell him you need a ride."

"You tell him," Lynn said.

"I have a ride," I said.

"Dummy. You tell him *I* need a ride. Okay? Please?"

"Actually, I already did," I said, grinning at her.

By that night everything was set. The plan was for the six of us to meet at the movie theater at seven o'clock. Jared and Lynn arrived the same time as Paul and I. Amy and Bill were late. We kept looking at our watches and at the crowd going into the theater. Finally Lynn and Jared went in to save seats. Laughing, I whispered to Lynn that her chances of sitting next to Jared were extremely good—that was one worry she could have skipped.

At last Bill and Amy were dropped off, and we saw that they were not alone. Behind Amy were her overweight younger sister, who was about eight and looked like Miss Piggy, and her skinny six-year-old brother, who looked like Kermit the Frog. "My mother said I had to bring my sister and brother, or I couldn't go. I *tried* to convince her to get a sitter, but she said she thought she already had one . . . me." Amy made a face.

"Don't worry," I said, looking at Amy more closely. "Amy," I whispered. "Do you know you have makeup on only one eye?"

"Oh, my God!" Amy squealed and put her hands to her

face. "We had such a scene at my house, I forgot what I was doing! Dana, can you watch Shelly and Hank for a minute while I run to the ladies' room?"

"Sure. We'll find our seats. Bill can wait for you."

Amy ran off toward the restroom, and I turned to herd Shelly and Hank into the theater. I hoped there would be enough seats.

"I never saw Amy move so fast," Paul said laughing. "Girls and makeup. Wouldn't it be easier to forget it?"

"You don't understand *or* appreciate what we go through," I said, batting my eyes at him. "Now, we've got to get these younger guys organized. Okay, Shelly and Hank, let's go find seats."

Shelly mumbled something and held up a dollar. Hank dug into his pocket and pulled one out, too. They both started toward the snack counter.

Again, Shelly said something. Then she pointed to the jumbo popcorn tub. "I don't think you have enough for the big one, Shelly, but you could have the medium-size one," I said. She scowled at me and said something to Hank. Why did she sound like she had mashed potatoes in her mouth?

Hank said he wanted Dots. His dollar covered that, and he was happy. But not Shelly. I think she had wanted Hank to chip in on the popcorn. She insisted that the jumbo tub was what she needed. Paul paid the difference so that we could get into the theater. Before Shelly took hold of the jumbo tub, she reached in her mouth and pulled out the biggest wad of gum I've ever seen a human chew. She let it drop, with a loud plunk, into the trash can.

"Okay, troops. Let's go," I said, directing Hank toward the door to the movie. Paul moved Shelly along in front of him. There weren't six seats next to Lynn and Jared, but

68

there were four in front of that row. Bill got Shelly and Hank settled there and went back to stand in the doorway to wait for Amy.

Paul usually has me go in the row first to sit, but this time he went first. I think he wanted to put himself between Jared and me. I leaned forward and talked to both Lynn and Jared, but I was careful to focus mainly on Lynn.

The coming attractions began. I always like that part. Then the opening credits came on the screen for the feature attraction. Amy and Bill sat down just in time. Amy turned and gave me the okay sign, so I knew she'd gotten her naked eye fixed.

I could feel Paul laughing. "What's so funny?" I asked, starting to laugh with him.

"Listen . . ." Then he pointed to Shelly. She was scraping the bottom of that jumbo popcorn tub even before the opening credits were finished! I couldn't believe she'd shoveled it in that fast. Skinny Hank was probably only on his second Dot. He'd better hang on to the box, I thought.

Behind us, I heard someone whisper, "Pow . . . Pow." I turned in time to see a kid I recognized from school flicking M&M's toward Bill's head. Bill turned and tossed back the wadded up wrapper from his straw. It was going to be a lively night. I glanced over at Lynn and Jared a few times and saw them laughing.

The movie was pretty good—a mixture of mystery and comedy. When it was over, we gathered outside to decide where to go for food. I knew Lynn and Amy were trying to figure where they could get the least messy, least embarrassing food to eat. I was pretty much past worrying about that with Paul.

Amy had to deal with her sister and brother. Shelly had

definite ideas about where to eat. She wanted a place that had ice-cream sundaes. Hank wanted a drink and didn't care where he got it.

Jared said we could all come back to his house. There was plenty of food and drinks there, although we'd have to stop for a sundae, if Shelly absolutely had to have one.

Jared led the way to his house. Bill, Amy, Shelly, and Hank rode with us since they had no car and Paul had the big station wagon. Paul was quiet driving over. "Did you like the movie?" I asked.

"Yup. It was pretty good," Paul answered.

"I loved it," Amy said. "Except whenever Shelly slurped her drink, I missed some lines . . . probably the funniest ones."

"There were some pretty good ones. Maybe we should see the whole thing again sometime, just us, Amy," Bill said. "No offense, anyone. But we both missed quite a lot. Hank had to be taken to the bathroom twice."

"Ice cream. I want ice cream," Shelly said.

"Shell, you had popcorn—tons of it—and a drink, plus some of Hank's Dots," Amy said. "I think you can survive on what Jared offers us." I heard Shelly sigh and mutter, but no one paid any attention.

"Paul, what do you think our chances are of winning on Monday?" Bill asked. He was a runner, too.

"Not bad. As long as Ted's knee holds out and the rest of us stay healthy, we should be competitive," Paul answered. He followed the MG and turned into the circular driveway in front of Jared's house.

"Whew! This is a big place," Bill said.

"I think my house would fit into this one three times,"

Amy remarked. "Hank and Shelly, remember—you are guests. So behave. And *don't* touch everything." Hank nodded. Shelly just stared back at her sister. I think she was angry about the sundae.

As we climbed out of the cars I heard Bill say, "It's pretty dark. Is anyone home?"

"I think my mother probably is. My Dad's in France," Jared said.

"No kidding," Bill said.

We walked up to the large carved door, which Jared opened without a key. If this were my house, I'd leave it locked, but a lot of wealthy people seem very casual. Inside, we stood in a front hallway. There was a long stairway to the side, leading upstairs, and overhead hung a huge chandelier. To the left was a very formal living room, and straight ahead was a corridor, probably to the den or kitchen. I could see from Lynn's face that she loved the place.

Jared called up the stairs, "Mom, I brought a few people over."

There wasn't any answer. "She must be asleep," Jared said.

He led us into the kitchen where he opened one of two refrigerators. "Help yourselves to the drinks. If you don't see what you want, there's more in the pantry. Amy, there's probably cake or something on the counter. You can see if there's anything your sister and brother would like." Then he opened a cupboard and took out pretzels, cashews, and bagel chips. "We can take all the stuff out to the barn. I have part of it fixed up." He turned to me, smiling, and added, "The rest of the barn is reserved."

71

Paul looked confused by the comment, but I explained that Jared wanted a horse. Lynn heard me and said, "Oh, neat!"

Paul laughed at Lynn. "You're about as comfortable on a horse as I am—admit it."

"Shhhh." She poked him playfully in the side. "Maybe the way to his heart is through a horse," she whispered.

"Let's hope not," Paul answered.

Chapter
Nine

"This place is great," Bill said as we walked into the barn. Everyone murmured in agreement. One side, where once there had been several box stalls, had been really cleaned up. Jared had taken out the divider between two stalls and moved in some old furniture, a rug, a stereo, some French posters, cushions, a bookcase, a space heater. There was even a phone.

"God, I'd do anything for this much privacy," Amy said wistfully. "I could be on the phone all the time and my parents wouldn't know."

"I sleep up there most of the time," Jared said, pointing to the loft.

Hank heard him say that and said, "Oh, wow. Can I go up? Hey, how do you get up?"

Jared pointed to the wooden ladder that was nailed in place. "If your sister says it's all right, you can climb up. Just be careful."

Hank ran to get permission. I wondered if overweight Shelly would want to make the climb. I felt sorry for any kid that chubby.

"I love that sleigh," I said, pointing to the other side of the barn, where several lawn and garden machines were stored. "Dashing through the snow . . ." I sang as I walked over to it. Knowing Jared wouldn't mind, I climbed into the seat and for a moment I could imagine swishing through a winter field, hearing only the jingling of the harness bells. "He gives his harness bells a shake . . ." Words from a Robert Frost poem ran through my head.

I was still in that snowy world when I heard Jared say, "It would be great to try this sleigh with Dusty some day, wouldn't it?"

I smiled. "Who knows? Maybe you'll try it with your own horse."

"I considered hitching it behind the MG once, but decided it would look extremely stupid," Jared said, laughing.

I whispered, "Stupid or not, let's try it sometime." I hesitated, then added, "Most people would think I was weird for saying this, but I'll risk it with you—this barn smells terrific."

"I know what you mean. It's the combination of hay, lawn machines, and memories of animals from the past—all mixed together," Jared said. "I'm not sure it's a smell that would appeal to everyone."

I looked over my shoulder at the others. Bill was climbing down from the loft ahead of Hank. Paul and Lynn were talking with Amy, who had a firm grip on Shelly's hand. We joined them and all settled into Jared's "living room" and talked and snacked for a while.

"I hate to be the poop of the group, but I have to get my brother and sister home," Amy said, looking at her watch.

"No problem. I'll drive you," Paul volunteered.

Lynn looked kind of pleased at the possibility of being alone with Jared for a while. Her curfews were as liberal as her allowance, so I knew she wouldn't have to go yet.

"Thanks very much, Jared," Paul said. I think he was trying to make up for the way he reacted when he found Jared in the tackroom. I was relieved to see that he was making the effort to be pleasant. It would be nice if they could be friends.

We dropped the others off. "Ahh . . . alone at last," Paul said, using a goofy, phony foreign accent. I smiled at him and leaned against his shoulder as he drove slowly toward my house. It was a really pretty autumn night, with a round, orange moon. When Paul turned the motor off in my driveway, he didn't move to get out—he just put his arms around me and said, "I'm really sorry, Dana. I know I've been acting stupid." He kissed my forehead. I wished the porch light were off; it was detracting from the moon.

"It's okay," I said, leaning against his chest. "I know I wouldn't be thrilled if suddenly some girl decided to be your pal. I guess I'd be pretty annoyed." Raising my head, I said, "But you'll just have to understand that nothing's happening." I thumped his knee for emphasis. "Zero."

"I believe you. I just wish *he* were more of a zero. But he isn't—he's an interesting guy, dammit."

I laughed. "So are you, dammit."

"Thanks for settling that. By the way, how was Rex's birthday? Did he get the card I sent?"

"Yes, and I know why you're grinning. I saw that card with the busty girl on it. Shame on you—corrupting a minor!" I gave Paul a playful punch.

"He's not such a little kid anymore. At least he doesn't want to think so," Paul said. "Where did your mother take Rex and his buddies tonight?"

"To some macho army movie and for pizza. Rex was really up for it, but Mom took some aspirin before they left," I said. "Speaking of Mom, she's probably pretty tired . . . not in the mood to have me come in late. What time is it?"

"Eleven twenty-five. Count-down time." Paul pulled me close again and kissed me gently. Then he looked at me seriously. I loved his eyes and the wonderful, worried eyebrows. "What are you thinking?" he asked.

I said the wrong thing. "Well, since Lynn's parents never worry about where she is, I was wondering how long she'll stay at the barn." I immediately saw by the change that came over Paul's face that I'd said a stupid thing.

"Come on—you mean you were thinking about Jared. Is he on your mind every second?" Paul said, annoyed.

"I don't believe we're back to this again." I sighed and fiddled with a button on my jacket for a moment. "Paul, by now you should know how I feel about you." I looked up at him. His eyebrows, that sometimes made him look worried even when he wasn't, were *definitely* making him look concerned now. "But if you're going to doubt my honesty, then I can't deal with you. Not tonight, anyway."

I opened the door and got out. "I was thinking about Lynn, not Jared," I said through the window. Then I turned and walked toward the house.

76

Chapter Ten

I had a rotten sleep. In the morning I didn't feel like getting out of bed. I just lay there stubbornly, with Pip curled by my knees. The phone rang at about ten.

"Dana—it's me. I think I've fallen flat on my heart." It was Lynn.

"What?"

"Jared is *so* great—I am *so* dullllll. He is *so* gorgeous—I am *so* blaghhh. He is *so* smart—I am *so* pea-brained. He is *so* . . ."

"Hold it! No one is allowed to talk about my pal Lynn that way. Not even you!" I said.

Lynn laughed. "Thanks, Dana. It's just that I feel so inferior . . . practically tacky. Me! Can you believe it?" Lynn rarely flipped out over a guy. Jared had really gotten to her.

"So what happened after we left?" I asked.

"Not as much as I wish. I mean, *what* a spot for a romantic situation." She paused, I guess to give me time to visualize it. I wasn't sure I wanted to. "Well, *I* could certainly see the whole scenario—right up to the part where he carries me to the loft."

I giggled. "Lynn, those were awfully steep steps, straight up. Tarzan would have trouble with that part of your scene."

"Details, details. Even if I had to be tossed over his shoulder, it would have been romantic. But . . . oh, I don't know . . . I just don't think I excited him much." She went on for a while, telling mostly how discouraged she felt.

"So what're you going to do today?" I said, changing the subject.

"I guess I'll just mope around here . . . you know, veg-out in front of the TV. Maybe overdose on junk food," Lynn said.

"I'll talk to you later then. Rex is yelling—something about doughnuts," I said. "Bye."

I wasn't making that up about Rex—he really was calling about doughnuts. I went downstairs to see what was going on. He was standing in the kitchen with a bakery bag in his hand. "Okay, okay, which one of you left me birthday doughnuts?" He grinned, first at Mom, then at me.

She shrugged and looked at me. I shrugged and looked at her.

"Come on, confess. Who done it?" Rex probed.

I laughed. "Really, Rex, I didn't."

"Neither did I," Mom said. "Who's left?" She leaned against the counter. "How about Paul?"

"I sort of doubt it," I said. "He said he had a lot of yard work to do today . . . unless he dropped them off early." I supposed Paul might do something to patch things up between us, or maybe just to be nice to Rex. But somehow leaving doughnuts didn't quite seem like his style.

"So, unbirthday boy, how'd your night out go?" I asked.

"Super movie. Great pizza. Fun night, eh, Mom?" He jabbed Mom in the side.

"It was a three-aspirin birthday, Dana. But I have another three hundred and sixty-four days to rest up before I have to face another one," Mom said.

"Well, who's going to be the first to try a doughnut?" I asked. "Are there any cream-filled?"

Rex opened the bag and peered in. After poking a couple he said, "Yeah, I think there's at least one. You can have it—I'll take the chocolate-coated one."

"Gag. How can you two eat such sweet stuff first thing? Are there any whole wheat in there?" Mom asked.

"Mom, if you're gonna have a doughnut, have a *real* one," Rex said.

The phone rang. "I'll get it," I said, heading to my room, in case it was Paul. I didn't want to talk to him in the kitchen.

"Hello?"

"Good morning," came the low voice on the other end. I recognized Jared instantly.

"Bonjour," I said cheerfully.

"Il faisait clair de lune . . ."

"Hold it," I broke in, "I take that 'bonjour' back! I never should have gotten you started. Wait . . . let me think . . . 'clair de lune' is moonlight, isn't it?"

"Oui," he said laughing. "It was moonlight . . ."

"It was? What was?" I started laughing, too. After my

79

last conversation with Paul, it felt good to be talking with a guy who made me laugh.

". . . that made me call," Jared said.

"Oh, stop, you crazy Frenchman," I said, "I know you're not serious."

"La pure vérité," he insisted.

"Ha."

"Ha, if you like. But anyway, I'm driving up to our country house later this morning and I'd like you to come. I'm leaving in about an hour."

"Really?"

"Really."

"Umm . . . I'm thinking if I can. It sounds nice. Hang on just a minute. Let me check." I went to talk to Mom, who needed a few more details but in general said it would probably be all right.

"Okay, Jared. As long as my mother knows where we'll be, and when we'll be back, it'll be all right." I got the information for Mom, hung up, and began to get ready.

Then worry set in. I thought about Paul, and about Lynn. How would they feel about this little trip? I considered calling Jared back and telling him I couldn't go. But then I thought about it some more. He was so much fun and *just* a friend, for God's sake. What would be the big deal? Paul didn't own me, and I was still angry that he'd acted so dumb last night. Lynn and Jared were only friends at this point, so it ought to be okay there. Besides, the idea of doing something new and different really appealed to me, and I needed a break.

While I got ready, I hashed it over and over. In the shower, it was, Should I go, or shouldn't I? Getting dressed, it was, Will someone get angry or not? Doing my hair, it was, Is this complicating my life?

By the time the doorbell rang, I had practically worn myself out thinking. I was sitting on the floor putting on my sneakers when I heard my mom say, "Hi, Jared, come in. It's nice to see you again," and I heard Rex ask if he could check out the MG. I pushed myself up, grabbed my sweatshirt off my bed, and walked downstairs.

"Hi. All set?" Jared asked, his bright eyes smiling.

"Yup," I answered, feeling better already.

"You two expect to be back around five or six o'clock?" Mom asked.

I looked at Jared to answer. "Yes, if that's all right," he said.

"Fine. But if you're going to be any later, please give me a call," Mom said. There have been plenty of times when I've been later than I thought I'd be, but usually, as long as I've called and checked in, it's been okay.

It felt wonderful driving with the top down. I felt free and unhassled as the fresh-smelling autumn air cooled my face. I wasn't very talkative at first, but Jared didn't seem to mind. Once I relaxed, I began to be more chatty. "You really have a wonderful place out in the barn. It must be peaceful there."

He nodded. "It is. And if you like peaceful, you'll love the country house. It's on a lake. It's the quietest, stillest— is that a real word?—place I've ever been." He smiled as he talked about it.

"Is there something you have to do there today, or are you just going for fun?"

"Both, really. My father left some things last time we

81

went, and he wrote asking me to get them. But it's so beautiful there in the fall, I wanted to stay awhile . . . and share it," Jared said. "Even the drive up is nice this time of year," he said, pointing to the brilliant colors of the trees.

I was reluctant to say anything about his driving, but I did. "Jared, you drive kind of fast. Do you know that?"

He slowed down. "Uh, do I know that? Well, the points on my license are a little reminder. I try to think about the speed limit, but I forget at times. Feel free to bring it up. I don't mind."

As we drove down the narrow dirt road toward the house, the lake sparkled in the background between the pines. We pulled up in front of a wonderfully casual-looking house. It was pretty large for a second home. "You don't have many neighbors, do you?" I said, looking around and breathing in the sweet pine smell.

"No."

"Do you have any at all?"

"I don't think so. Not close ones anyway."

It registered. "Do you own this whole area?"

He shrugged. "Guess so."

"The lake, too?" I asked. No one I'd ever met owned a lake. It seemed amazing to me, and maybe a little embarrassing to Jared, because he just nodded.

"We have a key hidden in the old well. Come on, I'll show you." We walked to where a pump stood by a covered boxlike structure. Jared lifted a wooden lid off the top and unhitched a rope that was secured to the side. Hand over hand he hoisted up a bucket attached to the end of the rope. Reaching inside the bucket, Jared pulled out a key and grinned. "Voilà!"

I peered down the shaft. "Isn't there water down there?"

"Not any more. It's dry. We use a different well," Jared said.

We went inside the house and instantly I loved it. Through large windows I looked down between the trees and out over the lake. There was a big porch with a hammock and large pieces of wicker furniture. The whole house had a woody, comfortable smell. "What a great porch," I commented.

Jared opened the door out to it. "You can sit here while I get the food from the car."

I was surprised that he'd brought food—I hadn't noticed it. But thinking about it now, I realized I was really hungry. I hadn't ever gotten around to having one of the mystery doughnuts.

Jared was right—this was about the stillest place I'd ever known. The only sounds I heard were the doors Jared was opening and closing, the call of a lake bird swimming below, and the creaking of the rocker I sat in. I leaned my head against the high back of the chair and closed my eyes as I rocked gently.

"Roast beef or ham?" Jared asked. I opened my eyes to see him standing over me holding a sandwich in each hand.

"Oh, I'm sorry. I almost rocked myself to sleep. Umm . . . which do you like best?"

"Either. You choose," he said.

"Let's each have half of each." I unwrapped the fat deli sandwich he handed me, taking half and passing the other back. "You were really nice to get this lunch."

"There's more," he said, reaching in the bag and bringing out a carton of salad. "I'll get some plates." He went into the house and came out with plates, forks, a bottle of wine, glasses, and napkins, all stuffed under his arms.

"Would you like some?" He held up the bottle.

Embarrassed, I said, "No, thank you." No one had ever offered me wine on a picnic before. A bottle of root beer maybe, or a can of Yoo-hoo. Was he used to more sophisticated girls? I suddenly felt very young and inexperienced.

He put his hand on my knee and grinned. "Somehow I knew you'd like something else," he said, pulling a can of orange soda out of his sweatshirt pocket. "Don't think I'm a lush or anything. I was brought up on wine with meals. But I'll share some of this soda today, if that's okay."

I nodded, relieved.

We ate, and laughed, and talked for a long time. Then Jared said we should go down by the water, so we cleaned up our lunch things and walked down to the lake, stepping over and around roots and rocks in the path. There was a dock where we sat, dangling our legs over the water.

"Don't you dare!" I squealed when Jared grabbed my shoulders and pretended he was going to push me in. "These are the only clothes I have!"

Jared let go his grip, but kept one arm over my shoulder while we sat there. We talked about favorite books and authors; I was impressed by how much he'd read, and not just that, but actually thought about what he read. Most kids my age just skimmed the surface. We also talked about what we hoped our futures would be like. Jared's family assumed he would enter the family business; that wasn't really what Jared wanted, but he hadn't figured out how to break it to his dad. Jared wanted to travel, working his way around the world for a few years. Then he wanted to write.

"Do you write now?" I asked.

He nodded. "I've done some plays and some short stories. Everything needs work, though. And I keep a journal fairly regularly . . . when I remember."

"Sometime I'd like to read some of the things you've done. Not the journal, of course," I said quickly. "Would you ever let me?"

"I think so." He looked at me intently, as if he was weighing trust.

I understood and said, "Maybe I'll show you some of my writing someday, too."

"All right. It's a deal. Want to take a walk?"

"Sure," I answered.

We took a path, not a very traveled one, which followed the shore line. I stopped to pick up some gnarled branches which had been drifting for a while before washing up against the bank. "I think I'll take some of these home and make something out of them—maybe a mobile. Tell me if you see any really unusual shapes." I knew the mobile would look good in Jared's barn. I'd give it to him as a surprise.

I spotted a branch caught in some tree roots which hung out into the water. Stepping out onto a rock, I reached, lost my balance, and started to slip. As Jared went to grab me, an image flashed in my mind. It was a scene I'd seen in films and read in books, where the guy grabs the girl just in time, then they look into each other's eyes, and finally they have an "unplanned," though passionate, embrace . . .

Chapter
Eleven

But that's not the way it happened. When I felt myself slipping, I shrieked, "Oh, noo!" and Jared reached and caught me before I fell into the lake. Then we both started laughing, and Jared called me some French word starting with "mal" that meant clumsy. Then he leaned out over the water, holding onto an overhanging limb, and knocked the wood toward me with his sneaker. I stretched and grabbed it.

"I hope this mobile's a good one, after all this!" Jared said.

"You'll see." I looked at him for only a quick moment, then had to look away, out of embarrassment. I had the strangest feeling that he'd read my mind and knew what I'd imagined. I felt so dumb. Why had I imagined it?

"Do you have enough wood yet?" Jared asked, hopping off the rock to shore.

"Almost," I said. "A couple more should do it." We

found three more interestingly twisted branches, then headed back for the house.

As we climbed the steps to the porch, Jared stopped and said, "I'm going to get my guitar. It's in the back of the car. Why don't you get comfortable? I'll be right back."

Gingerly I climbed into the hammock, half expecting to dump myself on the floor. It always amazes me that some people can handle hammocks so easily, while I, for some reason, usually flip over. I lay very still at first, until I built up my confidence enough to rock a little. By the time Jared returned with the guitar, I think I looked relaxed.

He tuned the guitar, then sang a couple of really pretty French songs. I think my favorite was one called "Plaisir d'Amour"; I asked Jared to sing it again. His low, rich voice was so nice to listen to . . . that was, until guilt began to set in. I'd managed to push it away until then. But there I was, like the Queen of Sheba, lying in a hammock by a lake, listening to French love songs.

I sat up, wobbled a bit, then got out of the hammock.

Jared stopped playing. "Anything wrong?" he asked, looking up at me.

"I thought maybe I should check on the time. I'm sorry—I didn't mean to interrupt your song," I said.

"Don't apologize . . . just be honest. Is there a problem?"

I shook my head. "No, I just thought that it might be getting late . . ."

"It's about four o'clock. Do you want to call your mother? We should be home in about an hour and a half, if we get ready to leave soon." Jared set his guitar down. "Or you could ask to stay a little longer—whatever you want to do is fine."

I walked to the railing and looked down at the lake. "This has been a really nice day. I love it here." I wasn't sure why, but I felt strangely sad. Maybe it had something to do with thinking I ought to keep some distance from Jared, but feeling drawn to him at the same time.

"And?" He walked over and stood next to me. I didn't say anything. Finally he said, "I'm glad you came."

"Me, too." I turned to him and smiled. "This is a wonderful place."

He nodded. "Maybe we should pack up. I think you're worrying about getting home." He put his hand on my shoulder. "But sit down with me for just a minute." We sat facing each other on a wicker couch.

"I will never intentionally hurt you. That's the truth," Jared said, looking deeply into my eyes. "When I saw you that first time in geometry, I knew in some unexplainable way that we were meant to be friends—maybe it started because you like horses, too—I don't know. I think it was more . . . a bond or understanding . . . I'm not sure, but something. You know it's there as well as I do."

I felt myself nodding, without meaning to.

"You know that there have been times when we've looked at each other and felt a closeness—" Jared looked away for a minute. "But your life was pretty full before I came along, and I don't want to complicate it."

"Jared, don't worry—"

"No," he replied, putting his hand over mine, "I do worry—not about a lot of things maybe, but important things. I'm not blind to how Paul feels, and I don't want to cause problems between you two."

I sighed, not saying anything for a minute. Then I said,

"I care about Paul very much. He's important to me. But . . ." I looked up at Jared. "I can't be afraid to get close to other people, can I? I ought to be able to have friends that are guys without it wrecking my relationship with Paul."

Jared's eyes studied me. "If Paul's having a problem sharing you, and if my friendship is causing you unhappiness, I'll back out of your life."

I shook my head. Even though he'd been in my life only a short while, I didn't like the thought of him not being in it.

"Okay, then, I'll try to be a Boy Scout—clean in thought, word, and deed."

We both started laughing. If ever there was someone who did not look like a Boy Scout, it was Jared. "Well, Scout . . ."

"You better not call me that *quite* yet." Jared winked. "I said '*try* to be.'" He stood up and held out his hands to me. "We should go." I reached up and he pulled me to my feet. "I'll get my father's papers while you lock the porch door." I could have used a hug right then, but I knew it was just as well he didn't give me one.

We collected our things, closed up the house, put the key back down the well, and left. I felt very relaxed on the way home. I could tell Jared was trying to remember about the speed limit because he kept glancing at the speedometer.

We chatted about all sorts of things. I brought up the subject of Lynn. "Did you have a good time with Lynn last night?"

"Sure. She's a fun person."

I looked at him and waited for more. He glanced at me. "Yes? What?"

"What do you really think of her?" I asked.

"Just what I said." He shrugged. "She's fun."

"Okay." I changed the subject and asked about France. Jared told me about his house there, and the schools, and his relatives. He asked me about my father and I explained the situation to him. Before we knew it, we were home.

We pulled into my driveway and I saw Paul's car parked there. "Uh-oh," I murmured.

"There shouldn't be any problem," Jared said calmly. "I'll go in with you." He started to open his door.

"No, Jared. I think it would be better if I just go alone. But thanks. I'm really glad you asked me to go with you today. I mean it." I got out. Jared reached into the back for my bag of driftwood and smiled as he handed it to me. "Thanks," I said. "See you." I walked to the house.

Paul was sitting at the kitchen table with Rex. Bernie and Pip both lay under the table, probably waiting to be fed.

"Hello, hello," I chirped with what must have sounded like forced cheerfulness. I set my bag of driftwood down by the door.

"Hi, Dana. Paul didn't bring the doughnuts this morning," said Rex. "So . . . who did?"

I was glad to be able to talk about doughnuts instead of about where I'd been. "Hmmm, sounds like a full-blown mystery to me." I walked over to Paul and put my arm on his shoulder. "Got any hunches?"

"Yeah," Paul answered, "but I'd rather not say."

So much for avoiding the subject of Jared.

"I'm going out to sit in Jared's car for a minute. I love that thing," Rex said. I knew Rex had no idea he was making things worse, but at that moment I wanted to kick him.

"He's leaving," I said, quickly switching to a new topic.

"Did the animals eat yet, Rex? They look hungry. And where's Mom?"

"Answer number one—no, they haven't eaten. And answer number two—she's upstairs reading," Rex said. Bernie got up and began to prance around the kitchen. He always knew when we were on the subject of his dinner. "Okay, okay. I'll feed you."

I turned to Paul. "How was your day?" As soon as I said it, I knew I'd set myself up for a reply I'd have just as soon skipped.

"Probably not as interesting as yours," he answered.

I ignored his sarcasm. "I have to go upstairs and talk to my mother for a minute—let her know I'm home. Be right back."

Climbing the stairs, I took several deep breaths to try to relax. I knew the worst was yet to come. Maybe I just ought to spend the rest of my life shut up in my room.

I walked down the hall to my mother's room. She was propped up against her pillows reading. "Hi, Mom. I'm back." She looked up over her glasses and gave me an understanding look. Mom has a pretty quick grasp of situations.

"Have a good time?"

"Yes . . . very. Jared's family has a gorgeous place on their own lake. And everything is so pretty in the fall." I plopped on the end of Mom's bed. "But . . ." I sighed.

She laid her book down. "I know—Paul's downstairs and now you have to deal with his jealousy."

"It's stupid, Mom, because Jared and I are just friends. It hasn't gone beyond that. He's such an interesting person. I should be allowed to have him as a friend, don't you think?"

"Yes. But life isn't that easy. Having friends of the opposite sex sometimes throws other people. A dashing, charming Frenchman who drives a white MG doesn't quite fit the buddy image. And think about it. If Jared were a girl, rather than a guy, and wanted to spend time with Paul, you might not be thrilled either."

"I know. I've thought about that. But Mom, what do I do? He *is* a guy, and he *does* like being with me . . . and I can't help that I like his friendship." I yanked on my sneaker lace and untied it. "The guilt is getting to me, though."

"I know. I can see that. You just have to weigh things."

"Know what makes things worse?"

"What?" Mom asked.

I yanked the other lace. "Lynn has a huge crush on Jared. But he doesn't seem too interested in her."

Mom grimaced. "Oooh. This is a fine mess, Dana McGarren." She smiled sympathetically. "All you can do, really, is to be as sensitive to everyone's feelings as you possibly can be. And that's the way you are anyway." Mom smiled at me.

"Thanks, Mom." I left and went slowly back downstairs. When I got to the kitchen, Paul was gone.

Chapter Twelve

I hurried to the door and saw Paul getting into his car. "Paul, wait a minute!" I called. He gave me kind of an expressionless look and stood by the car door.

"Where are you going?"

Paul shrugged and said, "Do you have time to see me now?"

I was becoming an expert at ignoring sarcasm. "Of course. Let's sit and talk."

We walked over to the apple tree and sat down under it. "You're angry—that's obvious," I said.

"You could have told me you were going off with Jared for the day."

"I would have, if I'd known ahead of time. It was spontaneous," I answered.

"So was my stopping over to see you, but my spontaneity didn't turn out as well as yours." Paul picked up a small stone and threw it at a tree trunk across the driveway. "Where'd you go, anyway?"

"Jared had to drive up to his family's country house to get something for his father, and he asked me to go—for company. I didn't realize doing that would turn into such a big deal. Sorry." I was starting to resent this whole situation. Explaining myself was suddenly making me furious. I turned and glared at Paul.

"Okay. Let's drop it," he said. I guess my glare got to him. "Anyway," he went on, "Alec is having some people over tonight. Want to go?"

"Fine."

"I'll come back and pick you up after dinner. How about seven-thirty?"

"Fine." I stood up. "I have to feed Dusty now. Then I want to take a shower."

Paul walked to the car. "I'll see you." He paused. "Dana?"

"Yeah?" I said, turning toward him.

"Forget how I acted. I worked all day and was tired. I got myself in a rotten mood. Don't take me seriously." Paul smiled weakly.

He was right—he did look tired. "Okay. See you later," I said, turning and walking toward the pasture.

It was a relief to be with Dusty. I stood next to him and buried my face in his mane. Then I went inside the tackroom and got Dusty's bridle.

I swung up bareback, and headed for the field across the road. When we reached the open stretch, I let Dusty take off and run. He galloped across to the path on the other side, and we headed into the woods. A branch whipped across my face, and another stung my shoulder, but I kept going. I pulled him up when we came to the brook and hopped off to splash cold stream water on my face. Sitting on the bank, I stared into the water. Jared's lake seemed to glimmer back at me.

My evening with Paul started out weird, almost formal. We were both trying so hard to act natural that it felt as if we were strangers. It was good that we were with other people.

At Alec's, everyone helped with the plans for Homecoming. Then, after we made a few posters, we watched a movie. Except for Amy and me, the kids there were juniors, but I'd gotten to know a lot of them, especially the ones in Paul's band, during the months I'd been seeing Paul.

Amy said something about how much her brother and sister liked Jared's barn, and I felt Paul stiffen next to me. When the subject got onto something else, Paul seemed okay again.

At about ten-thirty, Paul whispered to me that he'd like to leave.

We drove to a place near Paul's house where there had once been a large weekend home. It was owned by a wealthy family from New York. When it burned down, no one had gotten around to rebuilding it. The property was still very pretty, a nice place to walk.

We parked the car along the side of the long wooded driveway and got out. Paul reached for my hand and we walked to a hilltop overlooking the parkway.

"Let's sit here for a while," Paul said. He put his arm

around my shoulder and we looked up at the stars.

"I can never recognize many of the constellations—can you?" I said.

"Orion's belt and the Big Dipper are about all I ever make out, no matter how many of those dot-to-dot drawings I see." Paul leaned back on his elbows.

"Whoever made up most of them had a great imagination. But it's still nice. It gives people something to look for." I glanced back at Paul. It wasn't too dark to see how nice his eyes looked.

"With you under the stars, I don't need to look for anything else," Paul said, smiling at me.

I felt embarrassed, but good. "Thanks." I turned toward him. "I'm sorry about today. I didn't mean to get so angry."

"I didn't mean to get so jealous. I guess we're even. But really Dana, from my point of view, I don't see how a guy could take a beautiful girl like you up to a lake for a day, and not . . . well . . . not—"

"Paul, don't start again, *please*. He didn't do anything. And he won't," I said firmly. "I wouldn't have brought it up if I thought you'd start." I took a deep breath and tried to feel less annoyed. "Look, I'm flattered by what you're trying to say, and I understand how you feel. But everything's fine . . . and it will stay that way." I looked at the parkway and tried to figure out how to get off the subject before the rest of our night was shot. "Let's count pididdles."

Paul looked at me curiously. "What?"

"Pididdles—you know—cars with only one headlight. I'll kiss you for each one."

"That's an offer I can't refuse," Paul said. He grabbed me and gave me a kiss.

"Cheater," I said. "That was a motorcycle!"

"Didn't think you'd notice. Hey, you're cold. Here's my jacket." He put it around me and held me close.

It was like old times.

Chapter
Thirteen

The week before Homecoming was fun. Every day Alec's committee added a few more decorations to the school and made announcements about the upcoming event.

On Wednesday, walking to last period, Lynn said, "Jared hasn't asked me to the dance, but I'm pretty sure he hasn't asked anyone else. What do you think?"

"Umm, what do I think? You mean about going with him?"

"Yeah."

"If you want to ask him, do it. This is the age of equal rights. Be assertive," I said.

"Maybe you should kind of figure out how he feels about going . . . indirectly," Lynn added. "Could you?"

"Sure," I said, looking at Lynn's neck. "Hey, what's that mark?"

"Oh, that—that's my locker hickey," Lynn muttered. "I'm the only kid in school who can get a hickey from a locker."

"Tell me about this special relationship between you and your locker," I said.

Lynn rolled her eyes. "After lunch, I was at my locker, leaning forward with my backpack over one shoulder. The backpack slipped forward, hit the stupid locker door into my neck, leaving me with my head jammed inside. There is *no* way I did not look totally idiotic." Lynn started laughing.

I laughed too, then jumped aside as one of the biggest couples in the school strode down the hall. I don't mean big, as in big deal—I mean large. He's a fullback on the football team, and has no neck, and she plays sousaphone in the band. His large head was shaved like an egg, and hers was permed like a cauliflower. Lynn and I looked at each other and giggled. "Did you ever think what kind of kids they'd have if they got married?"

"Yup. Little tanks," Lynn said between giggles.

I hoped they didn't meet up with my favorite little teacher, Elwood P. Seeds. They could flatten him.

We reached the end of the hall, where we have to split up. "Don't forget to talk to Jared," Lynn called over her shoulder.

During band drill I thought about the dance. I was glad Paul's group was going to play. They hadn't played much yet this year and they're a lot of fun to listen to. Thinking of the dance gave me a really weird idea. If I could be cloned, I could go to the dance with both Paul and Jared. Boy, was that a greedy thought. Why'd I even think it?

While my mind was on things other than where I should be on the field, I suddenly realized that I was a lone mellophone in a sea of flags. Somehow I'd strayed into the drill-team area—I ran, dodged, ducked, and weaved my way back to my rank.

"Are you quite settled, Miss McGarren?" boomed the voice over the bullhorn.

I nodded meekly and decided to try to keep my mind on my marching. It wasn't altogether easy, because Robert, an overweight trombone player behind me, had on corduroy pants that kept making a "ssepp, ssepp" sound when his legs brushed together. I'd known him for years, and for years his pants have bothered me. When Robert was in seventh grade, he used to spit when he talked, because of his retainer. He had a crush on me and sent me a valentine with a truly memorable poem:

Bread is dry,
so is cheese.
What is a kiss
without a squeeze?

He scratched out the last two lines, and below it he substituted:

What good are your legs
without your knees?

Probably Robert would die if he knew that I'd remembered his poem all these years.

We reached the part of the program where Paul plays his solo. No matter how much my mind wandered during other parts of the show, I always paid attention when Paul played.

After practice, he kidded me about my mess-up during drill. "You were really marching to your own drummer, Dana."

"I know. Every so often my mind wanders during all that left/right/left/right business, and I just kind of space out.

Actually, I think band may be hazardous to my health. Besides getting foggy-brained from marching, I'm the only one who seems to have bees stalking me, and mouthpieces attacking me," I said. "But despite my calamities, I always listen to your solo and it's fantastic."

Paul put his instrument into its case and then into his band locker. "Thanks. Maybe the judges will think so, too." He grinned.

"My mom is coming to pick me up, so I'd better get out front and see if she's waiting," I said. "Talk to you later." I ran my hand over his back and gathered up my things.

Rex was in the car. "Hey, Dana. Did you ever ask Jared about the doughnuts? Maybe he's the one."

"I forgot to ask. I will, but I doubt it's him."

Rex shrugged and stuck his head out the window. His hair blew off his forehead and he looked like he did when he was a five-year-old.

The doughnut mystery was still with us. In fact, it was even more mysterious because new doughnut drops had been made. If they'd only been on weekends, I might have figured it was one of my friends. But we'd had two deliveries during the week, and kids my age don't have extra time to play practical jokes in the early hours before school. It was really strange.

When I got home, I called Jared to talk to him about Lynn. Before getting to that topic, I casually asked, "Do you know anything about doughnuts?"

"What? How to make them, you mean?" he asked.

"No. Do you deliver doughnuts to people in the morning?" I said directly.

"Are you crazy? I'm lucky if I get to school even close to

101

on time in the morning. I couldn't handle bakery deliveries, too. What are you talking about?"

As I explained the mystery, Jared started laughing. "Scotland Yard would never hire you, Dana. Think— think. Who is your culprit?"

"You mean you figured it out already? No way! And why do you say 'culprit'? Maybe it's just a very nice person."

Jared laughed. "I have a hunch, based on prior evidence. You should, too."

I knew Jared would tease me about this until I figured it out. "I'll come up with it—don't you worry. Just don't give me any clues, 'cause I don't need them." I laughed.

"I wasn't going to make it easy for you," Jared said, teasing. "Use that brain."

"I have something else to ask you about. Have you thought about the Homecoming Dance?"

"Not too much. Why?"

I hesitated for a moment, trying to plan my words so that it wouldn't sound like I was bugging him to take Lynn. "Well, it should be fun. The music will definitely be good. Paul's group is playing for part of the time."

"Uh-huh. Who else is going? The same gang that went to the movies?" Jared asked.

"Yup." It was awkward trying not to be obvious about Lynn. No matter what way I brought her name up, it would be clear what I was doing. I decided on a direct plunge. "You could—"

"I might go," Jared said before I could go on. "I was thinking of meeting one of my brothers in the city and going to a concert. But maybe I ought to do this thing."

"Ought to?" I asked, thinking it was an odd word choice.

"Yes, well, it would be good if I heard Paul's music and said some nice things," Jared said.

"You wouldn't have to try too hard to find something good to say."

"Oh, I know that. I've heard he's really talented. I just meant that it would be good if I were there to hear it and compliment him. I have a lot of respect for good musicians."

"You could—" I started to bring up Lynn once more, but again didn't get to finish. He must have been reading my mind.

"Is Lynn going with someone, do you know?" Jared asked. "If she is, there are others I might ask." I wondered who the others were.

He decided to ask Lynn. She would be so excited to find out I hadn't suggested it to Jared first, but to be honest, I felt a twinge of disappointment. Why? Because I hadn't had to push him into it? I was being silly. I changed the subject. "Hey, did you get those geometry proofs we have for tonight?" I asked.

"I usually don't do them. I've been getting by, more or less, on what I knew from my last course," Jared said.

"I'd be afraid—"

"Afraid of what? I ought to be able to spend time on what's important to me."

"Be realistic, Jared. You won't graduate without the right number of credits and without passing certain courses," I said.

"Relax. But while we're on the general subject of my delinquency, what's Mr. Warren like?" Jared asked casually.

103

"He's a guidance counselor. That's all I know. Why?" I started to worry more.

"No big deal. He's just requested the pleasure of my company in his office tomorrow, that's all."

"Do you think he wants to talk about colleges?" I asked, hoping that was it.

"More likely warning notices," Jared answered.

"Oh, Jared, already? You haven't been here that long. What could a notice be for?"

"Oh, just for an essay I haven't turned in for English. And history, for not doing a couple of assignments . . . But they were really idiotic ones. It was impossible to take them seriously," he said laughingly.

I sighed. "Jared, you have to do the work. You'll have problems if you don't. Your junior year's important."

"Sois tranquille, chère amie," he said in his gentle, low voice.

"But promise me—"

"No promises, Dana," he said, sounding serious. "I don't make them. That way people are less likely to be disappointed."

Chapter
Fourteen

In homeroom, Lynn was beaming. "He asked me!" She bounced as she told me about his phone call, and practically did cartwheels when I said I hadn't even had to suggest that he ask her.

"Hurray! Maybe now I'm getting somewhere. Okay, Dana, I think we should shop . . . and I'm talking serious shopping."

"What could there possibly be in any store out there that you don't already own?" I teased.

"Plenty. Major designers and manufacturers work around the clock just to keep ahead of me, I swear. This dance definitely calls for an entirely new outfit. When can you go?"

"Not today, but tomorrow after school. Maybe I can talk Mom into letting me buy something; I haven't gotten anything in a while. But even if I can't shop for me, I'll help you," I said.

*   *   *

It was obvious by Friday that it was a good thing the
dance was just a day away. Lynn was flying so high, she
was practically bouncing off the walls. I didn't know if she
could be contained for much longer. "When we shop this
afternoon, we want to get something sexy. Definitely allur-
ing."

I raised an eyebrow.

"Dana, face it. He's one of the sexiest boys in the school.
Everyone thinks so. Even with the hold Paul has on you, I
can't believe you haven't noticed," Lynn said. "The eyes,
the hair, the body, the clothes, the French phrases he
smoothly inserts at just the right moments. Even the sexy
way he doesn't do his geometry. My gosh, Dana, what
more do you want?"

"I don't want anything. I didn't even say anything."

"No need to get snitty. Just tell me—you spent a whole
day at his lake house without *really* looking at him?"

Quickly, a scene flashed in my head—the scene at the
lake with Jared when I was on the slippery rock. I'd imagined him grabbing me . . . and more. I'd felt embarrassed
then, and now for thinking it all over again.

I couldn't help feeling uncomfortable when Lynn was
trying on dresses after school and kept asking me which
outfit I thought would turn Jared on the most. After years
of friendship and shopping trips together, I suddenly felt
awkward.

Lynn settled on a dramatic red dress—low on the top
and short on the bottom. I got a light blue sweater dress
which was simpler and a lot less revealing. Lynn told me I'd
never be able to make a real statement wearing that kind of
thing. Maybe this wasn't the time to make a statement.

*　　*　　*

Saturday night Paul picked me up early for the dance. He had to get the instruments organized and help Alec with some last-minute details which Alec didn't dare leave to other committee members. Alec isn't the best at delegating. He doesn't have confidence that anyone else will do things right.

The DJ arrived just after we did and began unloading his sound equipment, each piece labeled with the professional name, "Intense Rhythm." Paul said he'd help him after he took in his own stuff. I asked Paul what I could carry and he handed me a small case. "I can carry more," I said.

Paul shook his head. "Nope, it'll help if you take that. I'll manage the rest." He's that way—I guess chivalrous is the word. A lot of guys aren't anymore.

After we'd set up for about twenty minutes, a few of Alec's committee members arrived. Bill was the ticket collector and stationed himself at the entrance. Amy and two other girls poured juices and soda and concocted until they'd made what they proclaimed was "superior punch." I tried it and didn't have the heart to tell them that it tasted like lip gloss. The other members of Paul's band arrived, and he decided they ought to find an empty classroom and run through their songs at least once. Paul apologized for leaving me.

The gym was starting to fill up and the DJ began the music. There were a few kids who'd graduated a year or two before. I know that's what Homecoming is all about, but somehow it seems that not many of those people actually come back.

There were some photographs on the wall of the sports teams, the band, cheerleaders, and people in the stands supporting school events. I wandered over to look at them. "Bon soir, ma chère et belle amie." Jared had come up behind me and touched me lightly in the back. Goose bumps tingled up my spine.

"You scared me! Sneak. I didn't see you and Lynn come in," I said, feeling as if I might be blushing.

"We just did. Lynn went to the ladies' room to do something to her hair. I'm afraid my car disassembled it." Jared chuckled. He glanced at the photos quickly, then turned to me. "Where's Paul?"

"Warming up with his band in a classroom."

"Ah, I see." He smiled at me. "You look beautiful, Dana."

That time I *knew* I blushed. "Thank you." I couldn't figure out what to say, so I fumbled ahead with, "Lynn's outfit is pretty striking. We shopped after school."

"You didn't really help her choose it, did you? It doesn't look like your taste," Jared said.

"How do you know what's my taste?"

"Easy," he grinned.

I scowled at him. "You think you know so much." I couldn't help laughing. "You're . . . supercilious, that's a good word for you—we had it in our last vocabulary unit. Arrogant, too."

"Sticks and stones . . ." Jared teased. He glanced toward the door. "Here comes Paul. Guess the band's warmed up." Jared leaned casually against the wall, hands in his pants pockets, as Paul walked toward us.

"All set?" I smiled at Paul.

"Yeah, I think so. Once we got going, it sounded pretty decent." He nodded at Jared. "Hi, Jared. Where's Lynn?"

108

"I had the top down in the MG and she got a bit blown apart. She should be out of the ladies' room soon."

"We're not on for a while yet, Dana," Paul said. "Let's get the dancing started. All right?"

"Sure. We'll see you, Jared," I said.

Paul and I danced and talked. Paul didn't say anything about Jared, and I didn't either. A lot of the time, we were talking and dancing with a bunch of kids at once. Lynn and Jared joined the group after a while. The DJ was good, and had an excellent sound system, but after the first hour, I began to get a headache. "Intense Rhythm" was pretty intense.

Alec picked up the microphone about halfway through the evening and announced that Paul's band was going to play, "for our listening pleasure."

They began with a fast jazz number called "Lullaby of Birdland," which everyone liked. Then they did a Dixieland number, followed by a really mellow song called "Midnight Sun." A lot of people slow-danced to that one.

Amy was upset about something and Lynn went out in the hall with her to talk. Jared walked over to me and said, "Would you like to dance?"

I hesitated. I must have looked pretty ridiculous, not answering.

Jared put out his hand and led me to a less crowded spot on the floor. When he put his arms around me, I felt myself jump, and when he pulled me very close, I felt as if a surge of electricity had shot through me. He danced well. I wasn't surprised; I was just furious at myself for feeling so idiotically nervous . . . and guilty.

"Paul's band is excellent," Jared said, sounding as if he meant it. "I figured I'd be impressed, and I am."

When the song was over, we walked back to where the others were and listened to more of the band's music. Amy and Lynn came in from the hall. Lynn whispered to me that Amy was upset with Bill for hardly dancing with her all night. Then she told me what a great dancer Jared was. I decided to keep my mouth shut.

When the band finished, Jared spoke to Paul. "Did I hear the influence of Clifford Brown and Pete Fountain in some of your arrangements? I liked what you did with that trumpet solo in the last piece. It had a Dizzy Gillespie sound."

Paul looked surprised, but not especially happy. "Right," he said. "I see you know music."

"A bit," Jared answered.

"Figures," Paul mumbled. "I'm sure you play, too. Talented as hell, I bet."

"Not particularly," Jared replied.

Paul muttered something under his breath.

"Paul—" I started.

He took my arm. "I could use your help packing up, Dana." From the glare Paul gave, I figured it wasn't a good time to argue. Lynn looked at us both with bewilderment.

As Paul turned and walked off, I shrugged and whispered, "Sorry."

"What's his problem?" I heard Lynn ask Jared, as I left to see what Paul wanted me to do. He was tossing music roughly into a box, then he snapped shut his trumpet case and handed it to me.

"Where are we taking these things?" I asked.

"To the car."

As we walked out of the building toward his car, I said, "Why are you acting like this?"

"Why?" He stopped and looked at me. "You actually have no idea?"

As he said that, I did have an idea and wished I hadn't asked. I knew I wouldn't like the answer.

"Was it necessary for you to dance with Jared while I was playing?"

"I didn't know you'd mind. You and I have danced with friends other times. What's the difference?"

"There's a hell of a difference, Dana. Face it, will you?" Paul practically spit the words at me. "You're involved with that guy even if you can't see it yourself."

I stared at Paul, not saying anything.

"You should have seen yourself with him." Paul let the box of music drop and took hold of my shoulders as if he were going to shake me, but he just gripped me and said, "I feel like a jerk, Dana. I don't know if I can put up with this anymore."

"What are you saying then?" I swallowed hard.

He looked away. "I don't know. I guess I'm saying it's about time for you to face things. Maybe you need time to figure things out. I guess I do, too."

I looked at him and nodded.

"I'm backing off for a while. You figure out what you want." He picked up the box and we walked silently to the car. I stood there as Paul put the things in the trunk. Then he turned to go back inside. "Coming?"

"I'll wait out here," I answered.

"Alec will think his dance was a bust if we go now. It's too early. I'll take you home at ten-thirty."

I looked at my watch. I had a half hour. We walked back

111

inside and I headed for the ladies' room. Staring at myself in the mirror, I wondered how long I could stay by myself without drawing attention. I thought about everyone in the gym.

I sighed and turned toward the door. Just get it over with, I told myself. A slow song was playing as I neared the gym and stepped into the doorway. I tried to pick out people I knew in the crowd of dancers. Amy and Bill were in one corner, and near them, by the refreshments, I could see Paul talking with friends. Acting as if nothing was wrong, the way he was doing, wouldn't work for me.

I walked back outside to wait in the car. Just as I was getting in, I looked toward the building and saw the silhouette of a boy in the doorway. Afraid it might be Jared, I got in quickly. If he saw me and came out to talk, there was no telling how Paul might react.

The car felt unfriendly as I sat waiting. Until then, I'd always liked that big family wagon . . . I'd often imagined myself with such a car when I had a family to drive around. But sitting in it alone, I felt its chill and emptiness.

"I thought you were going to stay until ten-thirty," Paul said, as he got in.

"I didn't feel too well. Besides, after you made that nasty remark to Jared in front of other people, and then stalked off, we couldn't have fooled people into thinking things were fine anyway. So there was no point," I answered.

Neither of us spoke a word the rest of the way home.

Chapter Fifteen

I lay in bed Sunday morning telling myself I ought to try to rest longer. Most of the night I'd spent thinking of Paul, Jared, and Lynn, resolving nothing, but knowing a lot was at stake. After staring at the branches outside my window for fifteen minutes, I decided to get up. I was on my way out the door to go downstairs to have some cereal when my phone rang. I guessed it was Lynn, wanting to talk to me about last night.

"Did I wake you?" Jared said softly.

I felt a rush inside. Swallowing, I answered weakly, "No, I couldn't sleep." I was glad to hear his voice, but after last night, I wondered if I'd be best off not hearing any male voice, except maybe Rex's, for a while.

"Are you all right? It got pretty tense last night."

"I'm okay."

"Good. Look . . . I know this may not be the best time, but if it's all right with you, I'd like to come over." He paused. "I'll bring you something. And I need a favor."

I hesitated, thinking that maybe I should be working on straightening out the mess I already had before going on and possibly complicating it more. But it was hard . . . he needed a favor and . . .

"Dana," Jared interrupted my thoughts. "It's a great day—all crisp and clear."

I weakened. "All right. See you soon."

I took my shower, fixed my hair in a French braid, and got dressed. I was just opening the refrigerator when Jared knocked on the door.

"Hi," I said. "I'm the only one up so far." I noticed that Jared had on a slate blue sweater almost the color of his jeans. From the way it was cut, I guessed it was made in France. I had to admit, I loved the way it looked on him.

Jared held up a bakery bag. "Croissants. I brought enough for your family, too."

"Detective McGarren notes that this bakery bag is not from the same bakery as the mystery doughnuts. You're not a suspect," I said.

"But the culprit is among us," Jared said, sounding intentionally creepy.

"You really know who it is?"

"A hunch, an educated guess. No doughnuts yet this morning, right?"

I looked out the door. Bernie shot through my legs and disappeared around the corner. "No sign of them."

"I doubt you'll get any today. It's too late for Sunday morning pilfering," he said matter-of-factly. "Okay, what'll we have with these croissants? Café au lait?"

"I think I'll have juice. But would you like me to make you some coffee?" I asked. "I think I know how."

114

"If it isn't any trouble," Jared said. Pip rubbed against his leg, and Jared leaned down to scratch him behind the ears. While I made the coffee, we talked, but neither of us brought up the incident at the dance. I did tell him I was surprised at how much he knew about jazz though, and he explained that his family liked music. It was one thing they all had in common. When his dad was home from business trips, he used music, mostly jazz, to relax. His mother was a very solitary person, Jared said, and spent most of her day in her sculptor's studio on the third floor. When Jared was up there with her, he listened to her classical music. His brothers and sister all had different tastes in music, so he'd been exposed to some of everything.

"I'd like to meet your family sometime," I remarked, as I poured the coffee.

We took a tray and went out on the back terrace. Jared was right—it was a great day. The leaves were brilliant and the air was cool and fresh. I could see Dusty grazing in the pasture.

My mother poked her head out the back door. "Well, good morning. I thought perhaps the croissants on the counter meant a visit from a Frenchman."

Jared smiled and waved. "Help yourself. Those are for you and Rex."

"Merci," Mom said.

"And there's some coffee, too, Mom."

Jared grinned at her. "Guaranteed to wake you up!"

"Ooops. Too strong, huh?" I said.

"I always wanted to have a hairy chest. This may do it," Jared said. "I'm only kidding. It's really fine."

The croissants were excellent, and certainly a nice

change from doughnuts. I loved having breakfast outside and wished I could remember to do it more often.

We were just putting things back onto the tray, when Bernie trotted across the yard carrying what looked like part of a newspaper. I whistled. He proudly presented me with his gift—the TV section of someone's Sunday paper.

"Well?" Jared said, looking at me with eyebrows raised.

"Well, what?" I stared back at him. Then I looked down at Bernie. "Ohhh . . . you think?" I said, pointing to Bernie.

Jared nodded. "First the boots, then doughnuts, now a paper. He's bringing you presents." Jared began to laugh. "I suppose we ought to figure out where he's filching things from. What's close by?"

"Umm—not much, really. But there's a corner confectionery a few blocks away. I wonder if he could be running over there and taking things," I said.

"Probably. I say we leave the rest of the case to Detective Rex and go visit Dusty. All right with you?"

Rex thought it was hysterically funny that Bernie was a delinquent. So did Mom, except that she figured she owed money to someone. She sent Rex to the corner store to investigate.

We walked up to the pasture and sat under a tree watching Dusty graze. After a moment, Jared said, "Dana, I'm sorry last night turned out so badly for you. I should have foreseen that and not asked you to dance."

I flicked some grass off the toe of my sneaker. "It wasn't your fault. I could have said no." I paused and thought for a moment, then added, "But I don't see why I should have."

"When we were at the lake, I said I didn't want to cause

problems for you. I meant it," Jared said. Then he turned to me and grinned. "But, mon Dieu, you're so damned cute!"

Suddenly self-conscious, I looked away, feeling myself redden. "Thank you." After a moment I said, "Don't blame yourself for anything. Paul and I just need to think through our relationship, that's all." I changed the subject. "Would you teach me how to play the guitar?"

"Avec plaisir, chère amie," Jared answered, picking up an acorn and tossing it into the air.

"Great. Let's start soon."

"Any time. Now—I have a favor to ask you. You are the president of Homework Anonymous, are you not?" Jared asked.

I laughed. "What?"

"The place to get moral support, a word of encouragement, a kick in the pants," Jared said.

"I'd be glad to give you a kick in the pants."

"How 'bout we mix pleasure and work? We could take Dusty for a ride to my barn, and then you could crack the whip a bit, so that I get some of those inane overdue assignments done?" Jared asked.

"You'll really do some work if I do?" I asked.

"Cross my heart."

"Okay. You saddle him up, and I'll get my books and a backpack to carry them in."

Dusty was in high spirits. He picked up his hooves and didn't even mind carrying us double. I jounced along behind Jared, my arms loosely around his waist. When we reached his barn, Jared pulled Dusty up. I pushed myself straight back and slid down over the rump and tail.

"We'll leave him over there," he said, pointing to the pasture next to his barn.

"Dusty is going to love that lush grass," I said, leading Dusty through the gate. We hung the saddle and bridle on the fence and turned him loose.

"We'll work in the barn," Jared said.

I took off my backpack of books and settled into an old chair. Jared spread his work out on the floor. I gave him a pep talk about being conscientious and it worked . . . for a while, anyway. We concentrated on our assignments for almost an hour. Then Jared stood up. "Break time!"

"Jared, sit," I said firmly. "You've got to get this done."

"I can only sit in one-hour intervals. One tiny break. I'll just go get us a drink," he said, backing out the door, then turning to dash to the house. A moment later he was back with two Cokes and a can of macadamia nuts.

"These nuts don't quite make it," Jared said. "What we really need are Reese's peanut butter cups."

Shaking my head, I said, "Give it up, Jared. You have no Reese's, so settle for the nuts. I'm going back to work now." I picked up my chemistry notebook and began to write.

Jared went back to his history, but after twenty minutes he was up again, pacing. He stopped and looked at me long and hard. I knew his wheels were turning. "Dana, Dusty's bored. He needs to go to town."

"Bored, my foot," I said, looking out the window at a horse blissfully grazing in Jared's field.

"He'll get fat. We can't have that," Jared said. He went to the door and whistled for Dusty, who looked up for a minute, then went back to eating.

"I'll feel like a cowhand riding into town on a horse . . ."

118

I began to protest, but Jared was already off getting the bridle.

Fifteen minutes later we were clopping down Main Street toward the newspaper store that stays open on Sundays. Since there was no hitching post, we used a lamppost. We tried to keep straight faces as we walked into the store. We could see people looking out at Dusty and back at us. Maybe they wondered if we were Amish.

I could feel a giggle starting in my stomach, and I knew if I didn't leave the store right away I would explode into laughter. Jared was calmly stacking Reese's cups into his hand, but giving me side glances and flicking his eyebrows at me, Groucho Marx fashion. I had to walk out.

"Dusty," I said, "you are making a spectacle of yourself." He turned his head and blinked his big brown eyes at me. I made a face at him. Jared came out and we clopped back out of town, with Jared sitting behind me holding a soda in one hand, and his candy in the other. As we turned up his driveway he swung around and rode backwards.

I laughed. "You're ridiculous!"

"There are worse things to be," Jared said, hopping to the ground as we neared the barn.

I thought for a moment. "That's true. And I'm probably some of those worse things." I was sure that Paul had thought of a few of them recently.

"Not so. You're some of the best things," Jared said.

I looked at him, curiously. "Like what?"

"You're like a smile," Jared said.

"Okay. You're like a wink!" I answered.

Jared laughed. "All right. You're like a refreshing drink of a very nice rosé wine."

"And you're like an energizing glass of Gatorade!"

After we got back to the barn, we worked for almost another hour. When Jared got up and began walking around again, I decided he'd probably done about as much as he was going to and I'd better be getting home. I began to gather my things together and put them in my backpack.

"Your car's at my house," I reminded him.

"I know. I think I'll pick it up in the morning and give you a ride to school."

Dusty was sorry to leave. The grazing must have been heavenly for him. "See how nice a horse looks here?" Jared said. "I was going to accelerate my campaign to get one, but I don't suppose the week that warning notices arrive home is the ideal time."

"Hardly," I said, laughing and turning Dusty down the driveway.

"Happy trails to you," Jared sang, doing a pretty good Roy Rogers imitation.

I whistled the next phrase over my shoulder.

I doubted he could hear me but it wouldn't matter. He'd know I answered.

When I got home, I took my bag of driftwood out to the garage and started to work on the mobile. I laid the pieces out on the floor and arranged them different ways. For the top piece, I decided on a gnarled root with lots of small shoots coming out from it. It was perfect for hanging other pieces from, using some of Rex's fish line. From those other pieces, I hung still smaller ones. The soaked and weathered wood was a soft gray, a lighter shade than when I had first fished most of it out of the lake. I hung the mobile from a nail in a rafter, leaned against the wall, and watched it turn for a while.

Mom was paying bills at her desk when I went upstairs. I peered into her room and waved. "How'd it go with Bernie the scamp? Did Rex go to the corner store?"

"Yes, and the owner said he had frequently been missing part of their doughnut delivery. I reimbursed him and promised to put up a fence for our transgressor. I guess that's the best way to be sure he stays where he belongs."

"Guess so," I agreed, but I knew Bernie would be annoyed. I leaned back against the door frame and chewed on a fingernail.

"Anything wrong?" Mom asked.

"I don't know . . . kind of."

"I think I can guess," Mom said. "The Paul and Jared situation. Getting sticky, right?"

"Yeah. Paul got really angry last night when I danced with Jared. I don't know how I feel about Paul right now. It seems as if maybe he expects me to make a choice or something."

"That's tough," Mom said, sympathetically. "I know how important your relationship with Paul has been, but I can see how Jared would be hard to resist."

I leaned over and picked up some cat fur off the floor. "Jared is so much fun and he makes me laugh, Mom. It's hard not to want to be with him, but it doesn't mean I don't want to be with Paul," I said.

Mom nodded. "These things aren't easy. Three wonderful people's feelings are involved."

121

"Four, if you count Lynn." I sighed and walked down the hall.

"Hi, Rex," I said, passing his room.

"Inverted, perverted, what's the difference," Rex grumbled.

"What are you talking about?" I said, backing up a few steps and looking in his room.

"Sentences. We have to identify types. The ones that are flipped around backwards are inverted, I guess. The rest I'm calling perverted," Rex said.

"I don't remember Mrs. Sterling having much sense of humor, Rex. If you need help later, I'll look at them," I said.

"Okay." Rex slapped his book shut and tossed it on the floor.

I started back down the hall and heard Rex call after me, "Lynn phoned. Call her back."

I groaned, knowing Lynn would want to talk about everything that happened last night. How long could I put it off, I wondered. It was hard for me to dodge a talk with Lynn after our years of closeness, but I wasn't ready to try to explain to someone else what I hadn't worked out myself.

Chapter
Sixteen

I heard the warning bell as I was getting out of Jared's car. Five minutes till homeroom. Before reaching into the backseat for my bag of gym clothes, I glanced at the front door. Paul was standing there.

I pushed the car door closed with my hip and turned back toward the school in time to see Paul walk away. He must have been waiting for me but left when he saw I was with Jared.

At lunchtime I sat with Lynn, Amy, and some other kids, rather than with Paul. It felt strange. A couple of times when I glanced at him, I caught him looking at me. When I stopped at the trash cans on my way out the door, Paul walked up and asked, "Do you want to talk later? After school?"

I did.

And I didn't.

But I finally said, "Okay. Where?"

"I'll meet you in the parking lot. My car's in the second row," Paul said, tipping his lunch tray and letting everything slide into the can.

"I'll just wait for you after band," I suggested.

Toward the end of band, my stomach started to tense up. I was feeling nervous about talking to Paul.

"I won't bite," he said as we walked across the parking lot to his car. "You can relax."

I nodded, but remembering how angry he'd been the last time we walked across the lot, the night of the dance, I wasn't so sure.

We drove to my house without either of us saying anything important. Paul turned off the engine and we sat silently for a few minutes. Then Paul said, "Look, Dana. I've been thinking a lot about us. What we've had together is good . . . special . . . and I'm not stupid enough to chuck it in the trash over another guy."

"Paul, Jared's not 'another guy' the way you probably think. He doesn't ask me on dates or anything. We're friends."

"Uh-huh." Paul paused, just looking at me. Then he went on. "But you two spend a lot of time together, it seems. And when you danced right under my nose, well, I felt . . . I don't know . . . I guess I felt like a joke."

"Like what?"

"A bad joke. You know—Mr. Nice Guy's too dumb to catch on."

I reached out and took his hand. "Paul, it wasn't anything like that, really. And you should know I'd never intentionally hurt you or make you feel dumb." I stared into his eyes. "You've got to know that."

"Yeah, okay." He sighed. After a moment he said, "Hey—"

"Hmmm?"

"We'll give each other space, but still do some things together," Paul said. "What do you think?"

I nodded, relieved at not having been pushed to choose. "Yes." After a moment I added, "I love spending time with you, Paul. Nothing has changed that."

We sat awhile longer, not talking. I hoped he understood that I wasn't turning away from him. Being with him was still very important to me; I loved the warmth and security I felt. And he was right about our having something special. But I couldn't make any promises where Jared was concerned. Jared's spontaneous, unpredictable nature drew me to him like a magnet—I knew that now. And I wasn't going to fight it anymore.

Chapter
Seventeen

It was the third week in November before I met any of Jared's family. One afternoon after school, Jared offered to drive me home and asked if I'd like to stop at his house first. We went up to the third floor. Jared knocked on the studio door, and when Mrs. Rochet opened it, I saw instantly where Jared had gotten his green eyes. She smiled and spoke politely for several minutes. Her voice was soft and low. It sounded almost as if she hadn't had to use it much. I admired her sculptures—birds, abstract shapes, vases, bowls. People, too—some complete, some just heads or torsos. I was pretty sure she had used Jared as a model for some of them.

When Jared and his mother talked, they combined French and English. I think if I hadn't been there it would have been all French, but they were trying not to exclude me. His mother's accent was very strong. I guessed she hadn't started living in this country until she was an adult.

Jared asked what they were having for dinner, and she answered with a French word.

"Did you ever have sweetbreads?" Jared asked. "What we're having is sort of like that."

"Sounds good. Like pastries, you mean?"

Jared laughed. "Not quite. We're having calf brain."

At first I wasn't sure whether to believe him—no one I knew ate brain. Jared's mother invited me to stay and try it. That was an offer I had serious second thoughts about.

I didn't want to be rude, but the idea of actually eating brain made me queasy. Explaining that I would have to call my mother to check on her dinner plans, I went downstairs to phone. Even though I whispered that I wasn't sure I could handle brain, my mother said she thought it would be "broadening" and "enriching" if I tried real French cooking. Some help she was.

Dinner wasn't for a while so we listened to music in the barn, then I went to the car for my backpack so that I could start an English essay on Thoreau. I wasn't sure how long it was going to take me to write it, so I decided to begin getting some thoughts organized. When I returned to the barn, Jared had turned off the stereo and was playing his guitar.

"You must think I'm a real grind to be doing homework now," I said.

Jared shook his head and continued to play softly. "Do what suits you and don't worry about it."

I smiled at him. I loved that he accepted and didn't judge. Sitting on the floor, and propping my notebook up on my knees, I began jotting down ideas.

Jared stopped playing, stood up and looked out the window. "Uh-oh," he murmured.

"What's the matter?"

"There's a phone company truck outside in front of the house."

"Yeah—and?"

"And you'd better go out there and stall them. I have to get rid of my phone," Jared said. I didn't get up right away. "Dana, really—go out there. All right? Distract them." He handed me his guitar and began tugging at a phone wire by the window.

"My gosh, Jared. What next?" I said, walking out the door, with the guitar still in my hand. "I don't believe this." I crunched down the gravel driveway, wondering what to say. The service man was looking up at the pole, then down at some papers on his clipboard. "Hi," I said. "Is the pole cracked or something?"

"Nope. We're getting an indication that there's something extra hooked up somewhere," he said, not looking up.

I twanged a guitar string. He looked at me, then back at the pole.

"How many phones are here?"

"This isn't my house. I was just walking out here." I twanged another string. "I thought I'd find a good spot to sit and play this guitar. It's a nice day to be outside, don't you think?"

He didn't answer. He just looked back up at the pole. Then he set his clipboard down and got ready to climb. Quickly I said, "Maybe the people across the street have something wrong with their phone, or wires. Those wires look loose and droopy. Maybe that's what's causing the trouble." I pointed across the street. He glanced in that direction, just as I caught a glimpse of Jared yanking a wire away from the side of the barn and running back toward the woods.

"Looks like an extra wire is coming off this pole," he said. I held my breath as he climbed. "Yup, this sure ain't the phone company's work." He snipped off a wire, let it drop, and started down. When the man leaned over to pick up his clipboard, I saw Jared sprint to the house.

The repair man started to follow the wire, until he got to the dead end of it lying a few yards from the barn. He picked up the end and looked at it. "This was cut pretty recently," he commented. I shrugged. "Is there a phone in this barn?"

"I don't live here." That was a truthful answer.

He walked toward the house and was about to ring the bell when Jared came to the door. "Is there a problem with our phone or something?" Jared said, with an innocent look of surprise on his face.

"I'd like to check in the barn," the phone man said.

"The barn? Certainly," Jared answered. I winced, afraid he'd sounded a little cocky.

The search turned up nothing. "The phone company does not allow private individuals to hook up to the utility pole. If you know of someone doing that, would you inform that individual? Thanks." The man stared hard at Jared and then strode off toward his truck. A few minutes later, he drove away.

I set the guitar down and collapsed onto the couch. "Oh, my God, Jared. That was unreal." I let out an enormous sigh. "What in the world did you do with your phone?"

"I threw it into the woods." He grinned at me. "Close call, huh? I guess I'll have to go about getting a phone the boring way."

"Boring isn't something you have to worry about," I said. "I feel like we're Bonnie and Clyde."

Jared tried to look shocked. "I haven't asked you to rob banks with me yet. That comes next week. We'll ride Dusty into town and . . ."

"Stop!" I scowled at him and tried not to laugh. "Did your mother see the phone company guy?"

"Don't think so," Jared answered. "She was in the kitchen."

Jared reached up to the top shelf of his bookshelf and took down a sketch pad. "Keep doing what you're doing."

I looked up, puzzled. "What are you doing?"

"Sketching you," he answered.

Embarrassed, I started to argue, "Jared—"

"Don't worry. I won't bother you. Just keep working. Ignore me."

"That's not easy. How'd you learn to draw?"

"When I spend time with my mother in her studio, I usually draw. I've never liked clay much, but I'm comfortable working with pencil."

As I leaned forward to write, my hair fell toward my face and I pushed it back behind my ears.

"Can you leave your hair free?" Jared asked.

I blushed and nodded.

He studied his drawing for a minute, then took his pencil and sketched some more. "Hmmm—hmmm, looking good, Ms. McGarren."

I couldn't help smiling. "I never guessed you could draw."

He winked at me. "I'm full of surprises."

That was the truth.

I tried to ignore what Jared was doing and went back to my essay. But my mind wouldn't stay on Thoreau and his peaceful, woodsy world. Instead it insisted on replaying that wacky phone company scene, which seemed to belong more in a Saturday morning cartoon than in my previously predictable life. Two months ago nothing like that would ever have happened . . . but now, with Jared in my world, I never knew what to expect. I was a little surprised at myself for seeing the humor in what he did before thinking about the fact that he was actually cheating the phone company. But somehow, his carefree way of doing things made me smile. He had his own style and it was pure Jared.

I glanced at him and saw he was still sketching. I stuck out my tongue.

"Be serious," he said.

"You're a fine one to talk."

Concentrating on anything with Jared sketching was next to impossible. When his mother called us, I was relieved . . . well, almost. If we'd been having hamburgers instead of brain, I'd have been more relieved.

"This sketch still isn't ready to be seen yet," Jared said, standing and putting it on a high shelf in his bookcase. "All set? Let's eat."

I took a deep breath and got up.

The table was set for three in the dining room. I realized that I should have offered to help in some way—set the table or something. As Jared pulled out his mother's chair and seated her, I felt a little awkward, not being sure if I should sit or what. But then he did the same for me.

It seemed likely that a maid would come through the

door any minute to serve the meal, but none did. The food was already on the table, and Mrs. Rochet passed each dish. There were small potatoes, peas, flaky rolls, and, of course, brain. There were also two glasses at each place, one with water, the other with red wine.

"This looks very good," I said politely. I wasn't lying really, because everything but the brain did look good.

"My mother is an excellent cook," Jared said.

I know Mrs. Rochet sensed that I was uneasy about the brain. She smiled at me and said, "Dana, we're happy you could be with us for dinner. Is this your first time trying brain?"

"Yes. How do you make it?" I wished instantly that I hadn't asked. I really didn't want to hear the details.

"Not difficult," she said. "First you soak the brain in cold water to be sure the blood drains out. Then you blanch it, then drain, then soak again, and remove the membrane . . ."

I couldn't listen anymore. It was all too much. I glanced at Jared, who was grinning. He knew full well that I was struggling and he was amused.

". . . and sauté in hot butter until brown, and serve with wine cream sauce," she finished.

I groped for something to say next. "Thank you for sharing that with me," didn't seem right, nor did, "I think I'll run right out and try that myself." I finally settled on repeating my first remark. "Looks very good."

I had some potato, some peas, some roll, some water, and even a sip of wine. Then I knew I couldn't postpone the brain any more. Cautiously I cut into my slice of brain with my fork and brought a tiny piece to my mouth. It felt smooth and almost velvety. If I hadn't known what it was I might even have been able to enjoy it. I managed to get through the meal, by joining in the conversation wherever I could, and taking tiny bites. I couldn't finish, but at least I hadn't been rude . . . and who knows, maybe the brain would make me smarter.

I asked if I could help clear, but Mrs. Rochet insisted I sit and talk with Jared. We had some very light pastries for dessert. I did my best to keep up with the discussion of a book both Jared and his mother had read. I hadn't actually read the book myself, but luckily I knew a little about the author. As I was leaving, Mrs. Rochet mentioned that the rest of the family would be home soon for the holidays, and she hoped I would be able to stop by and meet them. I'd like that, I told her.

When I talked to Lynn on the phone that night, she sounded angry that I'd been to Jared's for dinner. She muttered something about Paul.

"Paul and I have a different relationship now. I've told you that. But I'm sorry that my spending time with Jared is causing a problem," I said, meaning it.

"Well, God, Dana, you should be able to understand why."

"As I've said before, if he were a girl there'd be no problem. People are people, and half of them are the opposite sex, and we should not have to eliminate all of those from our circle of friends." Wow, I thought. That sounded pretty logical, even if I was the one to say it. Must have been the brain I had for dinner.

"You're making it sound so simple, and you know it isn't," Lynn said.

"You think I should see less of Jared. Right?"

"I didn't say that."

"But you think I should, don't you." I was getting more upset by the minute.

"Suit yourself," she said, coolly.

"That's what I plan to do."

We hung up.

I stared out my window. The shapes I used to recognize in the branches were definitely just a memory now . . . a memory of a much different time. Lynn had said I was trying to make things seem more simple than they really were. I hated to admit that she might be right.

Chapter Eighteen

My father called Thanksgiving morning to wish Rex and me a happy Thanksgiving. He was going to have dinner with his sister and her family. I was glad he had a nice place to go. Sometimes I try to remember holidays at our house before he left, but I can't very well. It was so long ago.

We were going to my grandparents' for Thanksgiving dinner and in the car on the way there, I thought about Jared's family at the lake. Jared had told me that they spent every holiday there except the summer ones. I could picture how pretty the table would look set in front of the large windows overlooking the water. There would be a fire in the fireplace which would make the house feel and smell cozy.

Rex took off his radio earphones and turned to me. "It *is* best to play a brass instrument, isn't it?"

"What?" It took me a moment to get on Rex's wavelength. "Oh—in the marching band, yes. Why?" I asked.

"I was just listening to my radio and I heard a trumpet, which made me think about my trumpet, which I'm not doing too well with, actually. I thought maybe drums . . ."

"What's wrong with your trumpet?"

"It makes my lips all sizzly when I play, and I get a headache from all that blowing," Rex said.

Mom turned and said, "It gets easier the more you practice, Rex. You really haven't given it much time."

"*That's* 'cause it makes my lips all sizzly and gives me a headache, Mom."

"If you ask Paul, I'm sure he'll take a look at it," I said. "Maybe it just needs valve oil to make it play better."

"I might like drums better."

"If you change instruments, you can't be sure of getting into the band in high school. They get more drummers than they need. But trumpets are always needed, so you'd definitely get in."

Rex put his headset back on and muttered, "Don't know if I can stand sizzling and headaching until then."

The rest of the trip was quiet. When we pulled into Gram's and Gramp's driveway, they hurried out the back door to greet us. Gram's hug was soft and powdery. Gramp smelled like Elwood P. Seeds' after-shave. Of course, Gramp didn't have the additional smell of the high school hallway to go with it, the way Elwood did.

The aroma when we walked in was fantastic. Everyone took a turn admiring the roasting turkey and proclaiming it the nicest ever. When we had caught up on everyone's news, Gramp sat down at his pump organ. It was the old-fashioned kind that had foot pedals to push the air into the bellows. The harder you pumped, the louder the noise.

There was an extra lever-type pedal that you pressed with your knee to give an extra loud boost to the music. My great-grandfather had owned the organ first, then it was passed down to my grandfather. I can't remember ever being at the house with Gramp and not singing around the organ. We sang all the verses of "We Gather Together," and of "Come, Ye Thankful People, Come." Then we sang the first verses of a few other Thanksgiving hymns which I didn't know as well.

"It'll be carols before we know it," Gramp said as he closed the cover to the keyboard.

I ate too much, and felt truly uncomfortable on the way home. I couldn't wait to get out of my dress, with its tight waist, and into something comfortable.

After I fed Dusty, I called Paul. I hadn't seen him in a while—he'd been out of school the last few days with the flu. "If I can get a ride over, would you like company?" I asked.

"Sure, but I don't want you to catch what I've got."

"Don't worry, I'll be fine."

"I'll pick you up in about an hour," Mom said, as I was getting out of the car. "Watch for me about nine-thirty."

"Okay." I walked up to the front door and rang the bell.

Paul's father let me in. "Hi, Dana. How was your Thanksgiving?"

"Very nice, thank you. And yours?" I was always on my most polite behavior around Paul's parents. They were very nice, but also a little formal. And I felt a little extra awkward now that Paul and I had a different relationship.

"Paul's in the den. You can go right in," his dad said.

I could hear the TV as I walked down the hall toward the den. Paul was sitting in a large recliner watching football. He had on two sweatshirts, jeans, and thick wool socks. A can of Coke was balanced on the arm of the chair. It was the first time I'd ever seen him not feeling well. Usually he looked as if he'd stepped out of a picture on a Wheaties box.

"Hi," I said, walking toward him.

"Careful, not too close," he warned.

I stopped in the middle of the room, then glanced around for someplace to sit. There was a footstool against the wall by Paul's aquarium. "If I can't sit with you, I'll sit with your fish," I joked. I sat down and smiled at Paul. "Well, did the turkey agree with you?"

"Not entirely," he admitted, "but Thanksgiving dinner is one meal I hate to miss."

"Are you really feeling better?"

"Yup. I'll give this one more day, then I'm done sitting around. Saturday I'm going to get some running in," Paul said.

I laughed. "Paul, are you afraid your body will turn all soft and mushy in just a couple days?"

"Getting out of shape happens faster than getting in shape. I can't stand myself flabby, and I want to go right from cross-country into winter track without having to condition myself again."

"Compared to you, I feel in sorry shape," I commented.

"Your shape is great," he kidded. "Anyway, you ride, and that's exercise."

I nodded, then peered into the aquarium. "Don't you have some new fish in here? Like that big googly one over there." I took a good look at his bulgy eyes and narrow mouth. "He reminds me of someone—I think the dentist I had when I was little."

Oddly, I was feeling a little uncomfortable. It was as if I had to keep up a lively conversation. I plunged on. "Remember a few weeks ago when Rex was asking you for advice about the girl he liked?"

Paul nodded. "Yeah. I suggested a few things to him."

"Well, he finally got up enough nerve to ask her to a movie. For moral support, he got his buddy Doug to ask someone out, too. I wish you could have been there last night to see him leave."

I described the two showers, the hour in front of the bathroom mirror, the gel in his hair, and the clothes flung all over his room as he searched for the ultimate "cool" outfit.

"How'd he look?" Paul asked.

"Frazzled. Doug's mother arrived early to pick him up. I went to the door to wave to Doug's mom, and nearly got run down as Rex flew past me, spit mouthwash into the shrubs, and jumped down the steps. It was lucky I heard him yell, 'Catch!'—otherwise I could have a black eye from a flying Listerine bottle. His last words were, 'Tell Mom not to talk too much when she picks us up.'"

Paul laughed. "Well, how'd the date turn out?"

"Memorable. Seems Rex wanted to impress his date, so he bought her a jumbo tub of buttered popcorn. Only when he went to hand her the popcorn, he bumped the arm of the seat and dumped the entire contents in her lap," I said. "Poor Rex. It'll probably be months before he tries the dating scene again."

"I'll talk to him," Paul said. "He's not the first guy to do

139

something like that on a date. I sat on a girl's purse and broke her glasses when I was that age. I swore I'd never ask another girl out till I was sure I could be more cool."

"You are now a master in the art of coolness," I kidded.

We talked for a few more minutes, then Paul glanced at the TV for an instant replay. Watching him, I began to have a nagging, unsettling feeling. Look, I told myself, be fair—he's sick. How can he be exciting when he's feeling like that? But if he weren't sick . . . would it be different? I closed my eyes for a second to try to block out my thoughts.

"Dana?" Paul asked. "You okay?"

"Yes. Fine." I tried to look perky to cover up. The fluorescent light over the aquarium flickered. "I think this light is starting to go."

"Yeah. It needs to be replaced," Paul said, reaching for his Coke. "Would you like something to drink?"

"No, thanks," I answered. But the truth was, I could have used some Gatorade . . . a sparkly, imported French variety.

Chapter
Nineteen

I pitchforked fresh straw into Dusty's stall and thought about the homework I'd left until the last minute. You never learn, McGarren, I said to myself, as I imagined the long hours I'd have to put in that night.

"Ahhh!" I squealed as I turned and bumped into Jared, who'd been standing quietly behind me without my knowing it. "What are you doing? You're supposed to be at the lake," I said, with practically no breath, as my pulse rushed.

"I'm back." He looked at me and winked. "Dana, what you need is a guitar lesson."

"Now?"

"You're tense. I can see it." He reached out and rubbed my shoulder gently. "Yup. As I suspected. Tight. What you need is musical relaxation, coupled with a horseback ride. Doctor Rochet's orders."

I tossed the pitchfork out the door into the manure pile.

"Jared, I want a guitar lesson, but I have a ton of home-work—no, make that three tons." I walked out of the stall and leaned back against the stable wall.

"But this is vacation," Jared said, taking a piece of straw out of my hair. "And we still have most of the day left. We're entitled."

"Jared—"

"Eh-eh-eh!" He held up his hand. "If we were meant to work, it wouldn't be called vacation. We need a complete break from the stresses and strains which school puts on us," Jared said persuasively.

I had to laugh. "Jared, what do you know about those stresses and strains—you don't do half the work you're supposed to."

"I'll ignore that, ma chère. I can see that academic pressures are weighing you down. And I am here to pick you up—I'm the spirit picker-upper." He took my arm.

"My spirits will be spinning in a panic tomorrow if I have to face my teachers with no work done and—"

Jared put his fingers to my lips. "Comme tu veux," he said softly, stepping back. "Don't get too tired, though. See you tomorrow." He waved over his shoulder and walked away.

The silence left me feeling empty. Instantly I missed the energy, the fun, even his voice . . . Oh, God, I loved being with him.

"Dusty, homework or no homework, we're going for a ride." I'd always wondered what it would be like pulling an all-nighter doing homework. I guessed I'd soon find out.

Jared didn't seem surprised when I rode up to the barn door on Dusty. He just smiled as we put Dusty in the field and then sat down with his guitar. The strings hurt my fingertips and I was amazed that he could play the way he did without being in real pain. I had to keep stopping and blowing on my fingers. Twang, puff, strum, puff . . .

I worked on the basic fingerings for nearly an hour. Twang, puff, strum, puff.

"Break time!" Jared said. "Your fingers need a rest, and Dusty wants to play."

I laughed. "The guitar? With his hooves?"

"Sure. No, dummy. He wants us to come out and relieve his boredom."

"You just can't take listening to my playing any longer. Admit it." I poked him in the arm.

"Mais non, c'est de l'harmonie céleste!"

"Hah. Not now, with all the puff-puffs, but give me a few weeks, Monsieur Rochet, and I'll be fabulous," I said.

"No doubt. In the meantime, I hear Dusty calling."

We walked out to the pasture where Dusty was grazing. "There's something I've always wanted to do," Jared said, grinning broadly. "Stand back, mademoiselle." He spread his arms dramatically, then slowly began to run toward Dusty's hind end. In a smooth motion, Jared placed his hands on Dusty's rump, and vaulted up onto the back of one very startled horse, who turned and looked at Jared as if to double-check what had just happened.

I clapped and said, "Bravo, but you're lucky you didn't get your teeth kicked out, Mr. Stuntman."

"Moi, Jared l'invincible? Jamais!"

Jared vaulted a few more times, and Dusty put up with it. Then Jared got the bridle and we rode double through the fields behind his house. As we rode Dusty slowly back to the barn, I leaned forward and rested my cheek against

Jared's back, feeling more at peace than I could ever remember.

It was getting late. "I have to go," I said, as I slipped off Dusty's back and walked to the barn to get the sweater I'd left there. Jared leaned against the barn door as I walked to the couch and picked up my sweater. He smiled as I neared him, then he held his arms open. I walked straight into them. We hugged, neither of us speaking for a moment. I wondered if he could feel my heart pounding.

"Dana?" Jared whispered.

"Hmmm?"

"I promised once I'd try to be a good Boy Scout . . . it's getting harder to keep that promise."

"I know," I answered softly.

We kissed. I never thought it was possible for one person to say so much to another in a kiss.

"You knew?"

I nodded. Then we laughed and held each other. I wished I could have stayed like that for always. I don't remember ever having felt so wonderful.

Jared took my hand and stepped back toward his room. I sighed and shook my head. "I can't stay, Jared, and it's hard enough to leave from here. From in there . . . well . . . no. I really have to go. Mom's probably holding dinner."

"Okay." Jared put his arm over my shoulder as we walked toward Dusty.

"One day after school I'll see if I can get a guitar book for beginners or something," I said.

"No, I'll give you some music. Don't bother to buy any," Jared said.

"All right, thank you. I've got to try to figure out a way

to toughen up my fingertips," I said, as Jared handed me the reins.

He leaned forward and kissed my fingers.

I caught my breath and swung up onto Dusty. Jared put his hand on my knee. "Have a nice ride back."

I gave his hand a quick squeeze.

"Don't speed," he said, winking.

Chapter
Twenty

The weeks before Christmas passed like a blur. With con-
certs, plays, tests, term papers, shopping, and decking the
halls, there was practically no time to think. Jared made me
find time to laugh, though.

Paul knew I was seeing a lot of Jared now. Sometimes he
made comments about it, and other times he seemed to be
trying not to. In school he changed some of his routes to
classes to avoid seeing Jared and me together. I tried to
make him realize that he was still very important to me and
to my whole family. He helped Rex with his trumpet in
time for Rex to manage his holiday concert music.

Teachers seemed to pile on work before the vacation, as if
they had to get it all covered then, just in case we never
came back after New Year's. That idea had strong appeal. I
was up late so many nights that when I actually got extra
sleep on weekends, my body wasn't used to it and I got a
headache.

Mom had to do a lot of the Christmas baking without me, but we did all manage to have one nice Sunday afternoon decorating the tree, listening to carols, and drinking eggnog.

At least I knew that some of vacation would be quiet, and that was fine, because I for one needed to crash. A lot of my friends were going away. Paul's family was going to Massachusetts, leaving the day before vacation began and coming home the day after Christmas. Lynn's parents were dragging her to Florida, but not to the fun part, and she wasn't thrilled about that. Jared was the only one of the three travelers who was happy. A few days after Christmas, he and his older brother, Adrien, were going skiing.

I exchanged gifts with Paul and with Lynn before they went away. Paul drove over with my present the night before he left. It was a gold bracelet with a musical note charm on it. He also had something for Rex—a new mouthpiece for his trumpet, which Paul said would make playing easier. I gave Paul a gray sweater.

The next day was our last one before vacation. Lynn and I exchanged our presents before homeroom. She gave me an electric blue scarf, hat, and mittens set, and I gave her an outrageous rhinestone pin for her jacket.

I hadn't seen Jared before homeroom. He was probably with either Mrs. O'Grady in the attendance office or Mr. Warren in guidance. They both earned their money in their regular dealings with Jared, but I knew they both enjoyed him.

After English, I spoke to my teacher about the reading we were assigned, kidding him that it was definitely a sit-up-in-a-hard-wooden-chair-book rather than a lie-on-the-couch-with-a-bag-of-chips-book. I liked that teacher a lot and worked hard in his class.

When I went into the hall, Jared was leaning against the wall waiting for me. "I'm going into the city after school. Want to come?"

"Hmmm . . . Yes," I said. "I probably can't, though. But, what the heck—I'll call and talk to Mom. What's to lose?" Nothing, it turned out. I called home between my next two classes, and miracle of miracles, Mom was in a fantastic mood, thanks to the Royal Flush Bathroom Remodeling Company. They had just come through with a lower-than-expected estimate to redo our upstairs bathroom, and Mom was really pleased. Any other day, she'd have given me a quick and final no, but today she was reasonable. She said that we were completely nuts, and that there'd be tons of traffic leaving the city. But after I explained that traffic didn't matter because we weren't in any rush, and that we really wanted to celebrate the beginning of vacation, she said yes. I would be forever grateful to the Royal Flush Bathroom Remodeling Company.

One hurdle over. Lynn was the next one. Even though she knew Jared and I were seeing a lot of each other, she would hate that I was going into the city with him. Maybe I could suggest to Jared that he ask her to go. I was pretty sure she couldn't because she was going away, but she might feel good about being invited.

I was standing by the phone booth, thinking, when Lynn came along grumbling, "I honestly *do not* want to fly to my aunt and uncle's house. It's too far to go to get to someplace where there's nothing to do. Really, Dana, have you ever been to one of those Florida retirement-type places?" She didn't wait for me to answer. I don't even know if she stopped long enough to take a breath. "I don't see why we always have to go to someone else's house every holiday. We're never home. I guess that's so my mother doesn't have to do any work."

"Your folks are picking you up after school?"

"Unfortunately. We're going right to the airport," she said.

"When are you coming back?"

"The twenty-sixth. My dad has to work. We'll only be there four days, thank goodness."

"At least you'll get a tan down there. Too bad you have to leave right away. I'm pretty sure Jared was going to see if you wanted to drive into the city," I said, trying to look as truthful as possible. Maybe a small untruth was better than a big hurt. I just hoped she wasn't too disappointed. I didn't know what else to do.

A few minutes later, as I was backing toward my French class, Jared called after me, "What? Ask her to go? Even though she can't?" He looked puzzled. "If you say so."

As we were driving down the parkway toward the city after school, Jared said, "What was that about Lynn? I asked, she couldn't, and what did that accomplish?"

"Well, Lynn is having a problem . . . ummm . . . I thought it might help things if you asked her to come today. She's a little upset . . ." I fumbled with the explanation. "I haven't been doing the right thing, she feels."

Jared laughed. "Right thing? *What* right thing? People make me laugh when they think they know what's the right thing for someone else."

149

"But she—"

"I know what you're going to say, Dana. She likes me. Paul likes you. You and I are close. Presto—a problem, a trite, little problem. *No.*"

"No?"

He shook his head. "No. I see it this way. I can't speak for others, but for me, it's like this—in my lifetime, there won't be very many people who will truly be close to me, and know me well. I'm sure of that."

I looked at his serious face as he drove. "I just don't believe that finding one of those people is a problem."

"But—"

"Look, you've been straight with everyone and you haven't closed them out. What's the problem?"

I smiled back at him. "I guess you're right. Hey, when did you realize Lynn liked you?"

Jared raised an eyebrow. "I'm not stupid, and Lynn isn't subtle."

"Some other girls like you too, I bet. I see them circling you, Monsieur Don Juan, in the halls," I teased.

"They're not subtle either." Jared laughed.

"Jared?"

"Hmmm?"

"Are you speeding, just a little?" I raised my eyebrows at him.

"Hardly at all. With my conscience sitting in the seat next to me, it's hard to be bad." He winked.

We drove down the West Side Highway to where the huge boats docked. "See that big French liner? That's what I came back from France on last summer. I learned the true meaning of leisure."

We parked downtown and walked to a store where Jared bought a lot of his music. While he was looking at sheet music for guitar, I walked over to the wall where several guitars were hanging. I plucked a few strings, then looked around to be sure I wasn't disturbing anyone.

When we were leaving the store, Jared said, "You need your own guitar."

"I'll put it on my wish list," I said.

"Do that." Jared put his arm around my shoulder, and we walked in the direction of the South Street Seaport, looking at holiday decorations in every window. "I'm getting hungry, aren't you?" Jared said. "I think we'd better stop and eat at a restaurant I know." It was French, of course. We were greeted warmly when we walked in. Jared ordered, since he knew what everything on the menu was, and during the meal several people came to our table and spoke to Jared in French. I heard his father's name mentioned several times. "Does your father eat here a lot?" I asked.

"When he's in the city." Jared hesitated, then he said, "My father and my uncle own this. I only came here because I didn't bring much money and . . ."

"You don't have to look apologetic, Jared. I'm glad to be here. Is there anything else your family owns that I can see?" I grinned at him.

"An office building wouldn't be too exciting. But you know, sometime we could stop there and let you pick out all the Rochet soap and perfume you want."

"Great. That would be fun. But really—about this restaurant—I doubt any other would be this good. I love it," I said.

"We don't have to have dessert here. I have enough money to go somewhere else. Have you ever been to the eating places above the Fulton Fish Market and tried any of the incredible food there? It's terrific."

"My treat. I have some money. Onward—"

"And upward? We could do the World Trade Center afterwards," Jared suggested.

I don't know if I'd ever had as much fun before as I had with Jared the rest of the afternoon. We sampled exotic desserts until we couldn't look at another thing to eat. We admired the decorations. We tried out gadgets and exercise equipment in some of the shops that specialize in unusual, and very expensive, things. We watched jugglers perform in the square, and we listened to a small band play Christmas carols. Finally we sat on the end of the dock and looked out over the bay. It was cold, but I was in too good a mood to care.

We just made it to the World Trade Center in time. They were about to take the last group up to the top, when we ran and managed to squeeze in the elevator. On the way up I got nervous that I might be sick. All the foreign delicacies were jumbling around in my stomach. I swallowed a lot and thought about other things to take my mind off it.

The view from the top made the trip up worth it. I was practically speechless at first, it was so amazing to be that high. Jared knew the city much better than I did, and he pointed out a lot of places I probably wouldn't have recognized without studying the maps. It had grown dark and the lights made the city sparkle.

I liked watching the other people looking out . . . and down. The expressions on their faces would have been wonderful to get on film. We talked with an elderly couple from Indiana, who had never been to New York, and with two little boys from Maine who were worried that the tower was blowing in the wind and might tumble over. The same thought had crossed my mind.

"Dum-da-dum-dum," hummed Jared, pointing uptown. "See the snakes of traffic leaving the city? We'll soon be a tiny vertebra in one of those long spinal columns. That's the price we'll have to pay for this."

"I, for one, say it's been worth it," I said.

"I, for two, agree."

The MG had a parking ticket on the windshield when we got back, but Jared wasn't concerned about it. He had a few others in the glove compartment and said he'd pay them all after Christmas.

We began our slow trip home. Actually, it was kind of fun to drive leisurely out of the city. I was able to get a good look at things. When we reached Riverdale, Jared pointed out a large stone house his family had once lived in when he was much younger.

"Are you cold?" Jared asked.

"Oh, you mean because we're riding in a convertible with the top down and it's December?" I said, laughing. No sooner had I said that, than a snowflake fell on my eyelash. "I don't believe this, Frosty."

Jared looked up and stuck out his tongue to catch a flake. "I love this, Dana." He poked me in the side. "Don't you? Smile!"

"I'm smiling. This is a unique ending to a great trip. But Jared, if it starts coming down really hard, do I have to shovel while you're driving? What does it take for you to put the top up?"

"A typhoon."

We made it home with just a light dusting of snow on us. But still, when my mother saw us drive in, she was right at the door. "I got worried when I saw the snow. How were the roads?"

"Not bad. The snow isn't sticking yet," Jared answered.

"You two must be cold. Want some cocoa?"

"Tempting, but I have to get home. One of my brothers is coming home today and my sister should be, too," Jared replied. "We have to pack up a lot of things to take to the lake house."

Mom closed the door, and I turned to Jared. "I'm glad I went with you."

"I am, too." He smiled and brushed a few snowflakes off my hair. "I have something to give you, but it's not with me."

"I have something for you, too. In fact, I should give it to you now. You may want to take it to the lake house."

"Hmmm, now I'm curious."

We got out of the MG and walked to the garage. "You got me a new car? How nice," Jared said, as we opened the door. I looked up and pointed to where the mobile hung. Jared put his arm around my waist. "It's great. I kidded you about this when we were getting the wood, but I knew that you'd do something really interesting with it. I like it very much." He kissed the top of my head.

"I've been wondering whether you'd want it in the barn, or at the lake house."

"The barn . . . because I'm there more. I'm going to hang it from the rafter over my bed in the loft. I'll look up and see you and me in that mobile, Dana—separate pieces moving their own ways, yet together."

"I never thought of it that way," I admitted. Maybe I'd learn to think more deeply as I spent more time with Jared.

Rex was sitting in the MG when we came out of the garage. "Hi, hope you don't mind, Jared. I just have this thing for your car."

"Enjoy, Rex," Jared said as he carefully lowered the mobile onto the backseat. "In a few more years you can drive it."

"You don't have a jacket on, Rex. Go inside. Scram," I said.

"Okay, okay. I'm outa here."

We stood by the car. "Well . . . have a great Christmas at the lake," I said. "I'll miss you, but I'll see you when you get back."

Jared smiled. "You have a great Christmas, too. I'll see you before I go skiing." He looked at me without saying anything for a moment, then leaned forward and kissed me. Then we hugged each other hard.

Chapter
Twenty-one

❧

Rex, Mom, and I went caroling on the hill in front of our church on Christmas Eve, a town tradition. On Christmas Day my grandparents came to our house. The morning after Christmas the Royal Flushers arrived. It was hard to believe that they had to achieve total destruction of the bathroom in order to improve it. Rex kept shouting, "Timber!" every time he heard a crash.

I baby-sat that afternoon. It was almost a relief to get away from the bathroom bashing.

When I got home, the phone rang as I was walking upstairs to my room. I dumped my jacket next to the bed and picked up the receiver.

"May I speak to Dana McGarren, please." The caller's voice made Jared flash into my mind.

"This is Dana."

"Dana, this is Adrien Rochet, Jared's brother." His voice was very much like Jared's. "My mother asked me . . . uh, she told me that you are a friend of my brother's. I'm sorry . . ." He seemed to be choking.

I felt confused and my stomach suddenly tightened.

"Jared had an accident this afternoon . . . driving back."

I quickly cut in. "Is he all right?"

Adrien seemed to swallow before answering. "His car skidded on some ice. He hit a tree."

"But he's all right?" I repeated. "Isn't he?"

"My brother . . . uh . . . he died instantly. Dana, my mother didn't want you to learn about it tomorrow in the newspaper. She said you were a good friend. Jared wouldn't want . . ." He couldn't finish.

I felt frozen inside. I wanted to hang up, to go back downstairs, and to walk up again, and not to have this phone call. I wanted to believe that this caller was not Adrien Rochet. "No," I heard myself say.

"Dana, it's terrible. I know . . . and I am so sorry to tell you." I can't remember if he said anything else.

I stood there staring at the wall for a long while. "No," I said again, shaking my head and covering my eyes with my hands, trying not to see Jared's car sliding into the tree. My head pounded.

My mother came into my room. She looked frightened when she saw me, and when I told her, she cried. I finally sank to the bed and sat holding my stomach and rocking back and forth while she rubbed my back. "No," I repeated over and over.

Except for when she left for a few minutes to get Rex to go to bed, Mom stayed with me all night. When I was finally exhausted enough to lie down, she lay next to me, with her arm over my shoulder.

I remember sitting up twice during the night. The image of the MG driving down the windy roads flashed in front of me. I wanted to scream for Jared to stop, to go back. I wanted to call to him to stay at the lake.

Sometime toward morning, I began to shake, then I cried so hard it hurt all over.

Chapter
Twenty-two

In the morning I knew I had to go Jared's house. I did not want to talk to my friends or see a newspaper. Mom had made breakfast for me while I took a shower, but I don't think I ate it. As I was getting out of the car in front of Jared's house, I looked down to see if I was dressed all right. I couldn't even remember deciding what to put on. A lot of my brain must have shut down.

Mom asked me if I'd like her to stay. I shook my head and told her I would call when I was ready to come home.

I stood on the front steps, not knowing what I would say when someone came to the door. A young man in his twenties opened the door. I told him who I was and he invited me inside, introducing himself as Jared's brother, Denis. I looked around the room for Jared's mother, but she wasn't there. Denis introduced me to his sister, Clare, and to his father, who were sitting together on a couch. There was some of Jared in each of their faces.

Mr. Rochet spoke first, almost as if he knew I wouldn't know what to say. "Losing someone you love is one of the hardest things. And losing someone who was so . . ." He stopped and shook his head.

"Dana?"

I looked up, knowing the voice was Adrien's. I hadn't heard him come into the room. He was almost a slightly older version of Jared, a little taller and more filled out. His eyes were very much like Jared's, only darker.

"Jared said some very nice things about you. And he had something for you. It's in his room." He put his hand on his father's shoulder and said, "Dad, excuse us, will you? There's something in the barn Jared wanted to give Dana."

On the way across the gravel driveway to the barn, I asked about his mother. Adrien's eyes filled as he told me she was devastated. Jared was the one in the family who had spent the most time with her.

Adrien swung open the large door to the barn and we walked in. Our footsteps echoed on the floor; the barn felt as empty as I did. An aching was growing inside me as we neared Jared's lower room where he'd played his music and done his writing.

"Jared talked about you," Adrien said. "He told me you were learning guitar and asked if I minded if he gave you the one he and I both learned on. It's a nice one. You should have it."

"But . . . maybe your sister will want to have it. Or you?" I asked.

Adrien reached down next to Jared's stereo and picked up a guitar case. "I don't play anymore. Probably I'll never get back to it. If I do, there will be other guitars. And my sister isn't interested in it. She plays piano," Adrien said, handing me the case.

I sat down on Jared's couch and lifted the cover of the guitar case.

"Jared polished the guitar for you and put on all new strings. Please accept it."

"You're sure?"

"Very sure. We still have the guitar Jared was using, which used to belong to my father. So there's one left in the family," Adrien said.

"It wasn't in. . . ?" I stopped, and swallowed hard, my eyes blurring as I thought of the MG.

"No. He didn't have it with him. It's at the lake house."

I nodded. "Thank you." I touched the polished wood and ran my finger gently down a string. "I'll never know anyone like Jared again. I am so sorry for your family," I said.

Adrien nodded. "You probably spent more time with Jared these past months than any of us did, except perhaps my mother. I know this is hard for you, too." Adrien looked up at the sound of a car on the gravel outside. He walked over to the barn window. "My aunt, uncle, and cousins just drove in, Dana. I should go out there."

"Is it all right if I stay here a little longer?" I asked.

"It's fine," Adrien answered. He turned and started across the floor toward the door. Even his walk was like Jared's.

"Adrien?" I hesitated, then said, "Why was Jared driving home yesterday? Were you getting ready to go skiing?" I had to ask, but I was so afraid of the answer.

He walked back toward me. "No, we weren't planning to

161

leave for a couple of days. Jared said that he was coming here for a while, and then he'd drive back to the lake. Dana, you know Jared had a will of his own and did what he felt he needed to. We don't know what he meant to do here. Just don't ever think it was your fault."

I swallowed hard and looked down. "Okay. Thank you."

"Dana? I think Jared was working on some music for you. Maybe it's in the guitar case. If not, I'll help you look another time."

I thanked Adrien again, and he left.

Carefully I lifted the guitar from the case and laid it beside me on the couch. I reached for the folder that lay in the case, untied the ribbon that was around it, and opened it. A card was clipped to some music:

Joyeux Noël, ma chère Dana—
I'll help you with these songs.
Love always, Jared

I felt so cold holding the note Jared had written when he was alive. He'd thought he'd be helping me with the songs. It seemed impossible that he was never going to be able to do that. Looking through the music, I could see what Jared had done. He'd written out simpler versions of songs he'd played for me and knew I liked. The first was "Plaisir d'Amour," which I'd first heard at the lake. The last song, which looked more difficult, was called "Dana." My throat tightened. Jared must have written it himself. I wondered if I could ever play it.

I leaned back against the cushions and sat with my eyes closed. Then I looked around. There was so much of Jared everywhere—the books, the music, even the Reese's candy wrappers. Jared's geometry book was on the floor by the table. I opened it. Stuck inside were some not-so-good quiz papers, along with some comical sketches and a limerick about Mr. Dougall.

I closed the book and stood up. I walked to the ladder and climbed to the loft. It looked as if Jared would be back soon—the bed was unmade, clothes lay about, a novel by Steinbeck rested face down next to the bed, a place held open. Oddly, I felt I should take the book home and finish it.

The aching welled up inside me again. I sat on Jared's bed and picked up one of his sweaters off the floor. It was the blue sweater he'd worn the morning he'd brought the croissants. I closed my eyes and buried my face in the wool, which still smelled like Jared.

Over Jared's bed, the mobile I'd made for him hung from a rafter and turned slowly. "Separate pieces moving their own ways, yet together . . ."

My mother came soon after I called her. I sat in the backseat so I'd have room to hold the guitar on my lap. Mom told me I'd had some phone calls while I'd been gone. I didn't say anything. I knew I couldn't talk to anyone about Jared yet.

"Did you speak to Mrs. Rochet?"

"No, she wasn't downstairs—not when I first got there, and not later when I went to say good-bye, after I'd been to the barn."

Mom shook her head. "That poor woman . . ."

As I was passing his bedroom, Rex called me in, and then

163

he hugged me hard. We hadn't hugged each other in a long while. He'd grown. "Dana, it's awful. Jared was . . . I don't know the right word," Rex said, looking up at me.

"I don't know the word for him either."

The phone rang a lot the rest of the day. Mom answered it and didn't bother me with messages. I knew she was telling people I'd get back to them when I could. I wondered when that would ever be.

After dinner, which no one could eat, the doorbell rang. Rex answered it.

"Dana," he called.

I froze. For one idiotic moment I imagined it could be Jared . . . that everything was a mistake . . . hadn't really happened.

I walked into the front hall and found Paul there talking quietly to Rex. He held out his arms to me and pulled me tight. Then we walked to the couch in the living room and sat down. He held me and stroked my hair. We didn't talk very much. I don't remember falling asleep, but I woke up on the couch in the morning, with my quilt over me.

Chapter
Twenty-three

The funeral was a blur. I guess it was a traditional cere-
mony, but I hadn't ever been to a funeral before, so I wasn't
sure. I just knew that Jared wouldn't have liked it very
much. If he'd had a choice about being there, he wouldn't
have been. But he didn't, and his closed casket was in the
front of the church by the altar.

My mother and I sat a couple rows behind the Rochets.
It was so hard to see them looking so destroyed. Jared's
mother had most of her face hidden by a hat and tinted
glasses.

Quite a few people from school came—kids, teachers,
even the principal. He was sitting with Mr. Warren from
guidance and Mrs. O'Grady from the attendance office.

Outside the church, my mother explained that the family
and some others would be going to the cemetery. I shook
my head. "I don't think I can do that, Mom. Is it all right if
I don't?"

"Perfectly all right," she answered.

Paul and Lynn came out of the church and down the steps toward me. "There are a lot of people here," Lynn said as she took my hand and squeezed gently. She had a lot of pain in her face. I knew if I hugged her we'd both start crying in front of everyone.

I nodded. Paul put his arm around my waist. "Most of the kids are planning to go back to the school auditorium. Even though it's vacation, they're opening for the afternoon and there's supposed to be some talk by the guidance department or something. What are you going to do, Dana?"

"I'm going home. Not to school," I said. I couldn't think of anything else to say.

My mom talked awhile—about what, I have no idea—then she said, "Ready, Dana?"

I guess Paul and Lynn went back to school. I hadn't asked what they were going to do. I hadn't wondered about much of anything in the past few days. How long would it be before I cared?

I walked up to see Dusty later. I hadn't even been to feed him in the past few days. Rex had done it for me.

Dusty was standing by the fence. He turned and whinnied softly when he saw me come up the hill. Then he trotted to meet me and nuzzled for the sugar I'd picked up without thinking.

In the tackroom, I stared at the brushes and currycombs lying in a row. My eyes fixed on the one Jared had brought. I stood fingering it for a moment before going out to groom Dusty. I began gently at first, then gradually I started to brush harder and harder. I got into a rhythm as I brushed, and brushed. Dusty turned his head and looked at me.

"Sorry, Dusty," I said. Then without understanding how it could have come out, I blurted, "Damn, Jared. Why'd you have to do that?" I began to brush hard again, barely seeing what I was doing though the blur of tears. "I have such an aching hole in me, Jared. So much went with you."

I walked out of the barn, wiping tears with the flat of my hand. Dusty followed me to the bottom of the pasture, then stood by the fence and watched as I crossed the road and walked into the woods on the other side. I didn't have any destination clear in my head but I followed the path which led to the stream. The ground was partially frozen, and as I neared the water I could see a thin layer of ice along the edge. I leaned against a tree and looked down to discover the brush still in my hand. I drew back my arm and thought about hurling the brush into the water.

My eyes closed and my arm fell to my side. I stood there for a while, remembering . . . "All right, Jared," I whispered. "I'm going to keep you with me . . . and maybe someday it won't hurt so much to remember."

Chapter
Twenty-four

I went back to school after vacation. Life seemed to be going on as usual around me; inside of me was another story. I plodded through my schedule, more like a robot than like me.

On our way to lunch, Lynn asked if she could walk home with me after school. I looked at her blankly. Was I supposed to be someplace then? I couldn't focus. Finally I said okay.

Paul saved a place at his lunch table and I sat down. "You all right?" he asked quietly, clearing a space for me on the table.

I nodded and changed the subject. "When does the marking period end?"

"A couple of weeks, I guess," Paul said. "Exams start the eighteenth."

Alec held out a sandwich bag full of oatmeal cookies. "Anyone want one? My mom sneaks wheat germ into these, so refrain if you are allergic to health food." Alec had been looking at me, I guess to see how I was doing. I was not going to dramatize the role of the mourning friend. Trying to act as if I had an appetite, I took a cookie and thanked him.

I don't know who was fooled, and who wasn't, by my behaving as if I were my old self. It didn't matter, I guess. I only knew I didn't want attention, and I also thought that maybe the sooner I acted okay, the sooner I'd be okay.

Lynn was quiet at first as we walked down South Avenue. Then she said, "Dana, I don't know if you can understand how bad I feel. First of all, I was crazy about Jared—maybe I didn't have the close bond with him that you had, but I really cared about him. On top of that, I feel so guilty. I was jealous and mean about your relationship with Jared. Saying I'm sorry now somehow doesn't make up for it."

I looked at Lynn's pained face, and I felt ashamed and selfish that I hadn't thought more about her feelings. How many other people had I ignored, I wondered. "I'm sorry I didn't think more about you, Lynn. I've been in a fog. I couldn't see, or feel, past myself. I know you cared for him, too. I'm really sorry."

"I just wanted you to know how crummy I feel that I tried to convince you to spend less time with Jared," Lynn said.

"Well, we're both sorry. I say we just move on," I said, putting my arm over her shoulder and giving her a squeeze.

It was a few more days before Paul brought up his feelings. He came over to spend Saturday evening at my house.

"Dana, I am really sorry about Jared. I hope you believe that I honestly am. And I'm sorry that I upset you by being envious."

"Lynn said she was, too. And it's okay . . . really."

Paul yanked on a loose thread hanging from his jeans pocket. He looked tired. "You and Jared seemed to have this easy understanding of each other, this tie between you. I admit that I hated that . . . really hated that. But I never wanted him to die."

I nodded.

Paul took my hand and held it in both of his. "I really detest myself for saying this—it's hard to admit—but I'm still a little jealous, Dana. Now Jared is going to have such a special . . . practically sacred, place in your heart. He didn't even screw up, the way I did when I acted badly. If he hadn't died, maybe he would have eventually; then he wouldn't be on a pedestal."

"He isn't on a pedestal, Paul. He certainly wasn't perfect, not by any means. You're right about his having a special place inside me, though. But so do you, and so will a lot of people I'll love during my life."

We all had our healing to do. It was slow as we tried to put our lives back together. I don't know about the others, but every day I thought about Jared, and I knew I'd never be the same person I was before he came.

It was a couple weeks later that I had a telephone call from Mrs. Rochet. I was surprised to hear from her and more surprised that she asked me if I could stop over and see her. Mom said she'd take me the next day.

All that night I kept wondering why Mrs. Rochet wanted to see me and what she would say. I worried that she wouldn't be all right and that I wouldn't know what to do to help her.

I chewed on a fingernail on the way to the Rochet house after school. Mom offered to sit in the car and wait for me, but I told her that I didn't know how long I'd be, so maybe she ought to go. I'd call later if I needed a ride.

I rang the bell. No one answered. Mrs. Rochet was probably up on the third floor. I rang a few more times, then I stepped back from the house and looked up toward the window just as the front door opened.

"I apologize for keeping you standing here, Dana. I had music on and didn't hear you at first, and then I had to come down from the top floor. Come in," Mrs. Rochet said. She was wearing a clay-stained smock and she looked better, at least better than she had the day of the funeral. Her eyes didn't have the same brightness they used to, but maybe in time that would come back.

The house was quiet—I guessed the others had left. Mrs. Rochet looked around and hesitated for a moment. "Dana, there is something in my studio I think you should have. I thought maybe I'd brought it downstairs earlier, but I don't see it," she said, glancing around one last time. "Would you come upstairs with me?"

I followed her up the wide, wooden stairway to the second floor, then up the narrower one to the third. She walked through the studio doorway and over to a table by the window. "Jared had been working on this before . . ." She held up the sketch he had started in the barn. "He wasn't completely finished, Dana, but nearly. I think it's very good."

I stood and stared dumbly at the drawing. Jared had

171

made me look so pretty. Mrs. Rochet held it out to me, and as I reached for it, I shook my head and whispered, "But it's so . . ."

She nodded. "That is you, Dana. Jared captured you very well."

"I'm not that . . ." I couldn't say it.

"Beautiful? That is the Dana that Jared saw. You are very lovely. Maybe it will take time for you to see in yourself what he saw." Mrs. Rochet's eyes filled with tears. "I want to thank you—you were such a good friend to Jared, and I am grateful." She turned away for a minute.

"Mrs. Rochet, I will never forget Jared."

She nodded and took my hand.

My mother didn't answer the phone when I called. Rex must have needed a ride somewhere. Jared's mother offered to drive me home, but I said that it wasn't very cold out and it would feel good to walk. With my sketch carefully wrapped, I set off down the driveway. At the road, I stopped and looked back at the barn for a minute. Then I walked down Chestnut Ridge Road, where all the houses were massive and sat on acres of property.

It was a nice afternoon and I thought about taking Dusty out for a ride. He'd really been neglected the past few weeks. Maybe Rex would like to come along for a run and take Bernie with him. Rex had gotten so much into running that he loved seeing how many miles a week he could total. Bernie, on the other hand, was into digging. He loved seeing how many holes a week he could total. A run might please them both.

I had another thought. Maybe I'd wait until after dinner and ride in the dark. I'd never done that, but it was something Jared would have liked.

The walk home took longer than I thought, but I finally turned up my driveway. I stopped by the dormant flower bed and flicked a few stones back into the driveway. As I was straightening up, I heard a car coming down the road. I turned to look just as it was passing. It was a sports car, but not white, and not with its top down. I supposed I'd be noticing things like that for a long time.